Romantic Love

রোমাঞ্চকর ভালোবাসা

NK Mondal

ISBN 978-93-5458-810-5
© NK Mondal 2021
Published in India 2021 by Pencil

A brand of
One Point Six Technologies Pvt. Ltd.
123, Building J2, Shram Seva Premises,
Wadala Truck Terminal, Wadala (E)
Mumbai 400037, Maharashtra, INDIA
E connect@thepencilapp.com
W www.thepencilapp.com

Author biography

NK Mondal is an Indian poet, social consultant, social and humanitarian activist, humanist, columnist, novelist, philosopher and writer. He was born in 1997 in the village of Pratappur in the Hariharpara block of Murshidabad district in the Indian state of West Bengal to a poor Muslim family. Although his birth name is Selim Sheikh, he is better known in the world as NK Mondal. In 2019, he was awarded the title of Sahitya Ratna. Father Saiful Sheikh and mother Menuka Bibi. Although the beloved writer had a good education, he had to face ridicule, slander, oppression and even death threats from various religious people. He has set an example in the area as a very honest and just person from a young age, yet he is humiliated by the pious. Because the author is a true Islamic, Despite repeated threats to speak out against misconceptions and violent laws, he continues to write with courage. Although he is a writer, he is actually a philosopher and has many talents. Although he is Islamic, he continues to write about theism, atheism, religion, society, country, movement, free thought, etc. Notable books are Love, The Ideal Human, Misconceptions and Orthodoxy, Beautiful Daughters, etc.

CONTENTS

Chapter 1

Green village of Bengal. The paths and ghats of Bengal are all beautiful. More beautiful village people's minds. Ordinary Bhola is a good man. There are no such evil people. There are some educated. There are some current intrigues. Again, the number of bad people is higher in many villages. Thamathampur is one such village. It is difficult to say where such work is not done. The village is surrounded by Hindus and Muslims. Seventy percent of the Muslims there. Thirty percent Hindus. Great similarity between Hindus and Muslims in that respect. No hassle. Trouble. Fifty percent Hindus live in Parliament No. 10. And fifty percent Muslim. Another parliament, the eleventh parliament, is surrounded by one hundred percent Muslims. Markets, banks, schools, ration shops and main travel centers in Parliament No. 10. Eleventh Parliament Field. However, the river Bhairab flows by. But he does not have water in the river. If there is water all year round, there are lots of fish. And there was a lot of fish in the field. Superstition in the Muslim society of the village, Always involved in violence and conflict. Muslims are a kind of big jealousy. It is difficult to go to Sheikh Para. Violence and violence. Admitted to political bullying. There is a Muslim society. But the work of Islam is more important than useless. Preaching is done every evening. That is, it gives Islamic invitation. Some good people among Muslims. They want to make the society better. But because it is full of bad people. Do not want to come to a better way easily. Now, of course, a few have joined the team. There are plenty of usurers in the village. It is difficult to calculate. Which is the custom of Hindu society. Now it is a big business in this village. Some Vicarians have also become rich. Nahid lives in Sheikh Para. The only son of the parents. There is also a sister. But small. The age will be around six to seven. Just a second grader. Good at studying too. There is a saying that if the family is good, the children are also good. Nahid will now be eighteen or nineteen. Higher secondary student of Thamathampur High School. Good results Every year. He loves the village more. Then Rina K. Rina is the daughter of Ramzan Matabbar. Kuchute Matbar. But it's a lot better. Nobody knows that. The mind is soft but it is hard to rule. Along with the good people of the village hate him. Among them is Nahid's father. Nahid's father is a poorly educated man. But there is no mold on the head. Poor people. But many people now take knowledge from him.

(2)

That day was Saturday. Rina has been dressing herself since evening. The work does not work. Matabbar's daughter. Rina is a very modern and smart girl. Looking at himself in the mirror again and again. And a lot of new punishments are being put in the face. Illusion HT, applied and freshened the face once. He combed his hair. He went to his mother and tied her hair. Came home again. There was a cupboard by the window. Mahalakshi Alta took it from there. There was a brush in the bottle. He put the brush on his feet as per his mind. After many glass bangles he looked at himself in the mirror again. Now Rina and Rina are gone. Now she is a goddess of beautiful women. What looks great. The eyes seem to be covering. It was as if he was thinking with his hand on his cheek. It is as if the soul is about to fly away. Looking back, the mobile is bent on the table. Rina said, oh now who again. There is no work by eating while thinking phone. He crouched down and looked. The text on the skin of the mobile has floated " How are you The opposite replied. What are you laughing at? Hey, where are the smiles? I don't understand. You notice that. Yes there is go go. I have just done this. You can come. You trust me. I don't think the opposite because I have. All right, I'll be standing in Matin's mango orchard. You only have to walk a couple of minutes. I can go. You don't have to worry. You just have to be more discriminating with the help you render toward other people. Nahid left the phone saying it was okay. Nahid and Rina are in love. Loves so much that no one leaves anyone. Some of the boys even tried to confuse Rina by misleading her. Sujan of that neighborhood. Sujan also loves Rina very much. He said. Rina, you have something to say. Yes, tell me what to say. I don't mean that it can't be said here anymore. It's an open space. So where do you want to say. I mean, it's better to say it in secret. Why in secret. No, that's an important thing. Oh. All right. Come to our house. Oh father, if your father sees you once, he won't keep me awake. Needless to say, if not here. All right, listen. I'm saying you're good. I don't remember anything, Rina. Tell me. Don't mind. The thing is, Nahid Rahman is having an affair with his cousin's daughter. You're wrong to recognize him, Rina. There is still time. Hate Nahid. The boy is not good. After saying that, Rina glowed purple in oil. He said you got me crazy. I will accept whatever you say. Even if Nahid flirts with a hundred girls, he still takes my toll. Not even in front of me. You move away from me right now. Otherwise I will take care of you. I want to remove Nahid from me. I don't know you What can you do to get me? Listen. I, As long as this Rina is alive, Nahid is mine. I will have. No one can take it. If you don't like me on the bus, I have no problem. I will live with the memory of love for the rest of my life. This time. Move that from in front of me.

(3)

The evening is over. The village is drowning in darkness. There is no light in the village roads. As a result, it is darker. Everyone in the house has fallen asleep. A few dogs are calling. The squeaking insects are squeaking. The head is getting worse. Suddenly a cringe cringe message came on the mobile. I'm gone. Where are you? I'm at home. Just leaving. Wait. Excluding the message reply, he came out through the back gate. There is a pond in front of the house. You have to dive. Moreover, there is another path which is the main path of the village. You can't go there. Because someone can see. So the pond has to be crossed. There is no water in the pond. A few days ago the lesson was dipped in water. One to two minutes walk after crossing the pond. Small jungle path. After crossing the road, Nahid was finally seen. Nahid is standing with a red ladies bicycle under a lame mango tree. Exactly the appearance of the city Like a king. What's the matter with you taking so long to come. See how long it takes to be born a girl. No, no, you don't have to stab. Don't tell me what to eat today. You tell me what to eat. No you say. If I can't eat anything. If I can't fulfill any of your wishes. But will you love me? What are you saying backwards. Even if you can't give anything, I'm always yours. No one else. True. Yes go yes. I will buy whatever you eat. I don't know all that. Buy me a beautiful doll today. Will. All right, no more talking, sit down. It's getting late. Boxiganj has to go a long way. Eight kilometers. It must be seven o'clock at night to go. Rina said, I can't stay long. I'll be there in about an hour. It will happen. All right. You cover your face well. Otherwise many people of the village will be at the fair. Can take a look. Mild winter nights. It's a lot of fun. There are people in love with. How beautiful it looks. And after a while they will be able to reach the fair in Boxiganj. Well, Rina, if the people in your house are looking for you. Then I will get in trouble. Not so. He must read. I'm not a boy, I will not be in trouble. What will you do. What else to do. You are My last hope. That's right. This is here. Rina, you do one thing. What work. Stand there in the dim light. I am leaving the bicycle in the garage. All right, go. Nahid left his bicycle in the garage and came to Rina. Come on madam. Which way to go. You say Let's have coffee first. See you later. Cycling is making your body cold. Come on. Nahid went to the coffee house and said. Excuse me brother. Give two medium coffees. We are sitting at the table in that corner. The coffee arrived in a few minutes. I started eating it. There are some personal conversations between the two while eating. Rina said I finished eating. I'm coming with the bill. Hey you mean pay the bill. I'm bringing it to you. I'll pay the bill. No, I'm giving. You save the money will be spent after marriage. How. Nahid laughed for a while. This is a kind of girl Ray Baba. Another girl explodes with her boyfriend's money. And Rina is completely different. As long as the relationship has been. Everything costs him. Really the girl Many beautiful minded people. He does not like bad deeds at all without good deeds. Rina came with the bill and said. What's the matter, what are you thinking. This is Mr. Let's go. Oh yes. Now I will look around the fair. Will not Why not. Come to see. Not so. Yes, Mister, yes. The two of them proceeded towards the main fair in Boxiganj. Boxiganj is a city-like place. Good place. About eight kilometers from Thamathampur. What's not there. Everything is available. He also comes here occasionally to shoot movies from Kolkata. Exciting place. Colleges, libraries, hospitals, restaurants, good markets. The whole market is illuminated. Looking at the village, no one can think that it is a village. Nahid said, That's Nila. You can see Rina. Yes, I can. Call him. Giving. Nahid dialed the number on his mobile phone. Nilar's mobile rang loudly. Nila said over the phone. What's the matter, sir? Phone this time. That's me again. I understand I can't call. Of course he can. Nahid pointed at Nilar saying that we can see you. Seeing Nila too, he waved his hand. And kept coming towards Nahid.

(4)

Nila is a classmate of Rina and Nahid. This is his home. A very beautiful girl. The pair is fair. The father's only daughter. The parents were married in love. Nilar's family is well educated. He lives in this village. It would not be right to call it a village. The city has to say. Because there is no. All available. Nila came and said. You are here. Tonight. What's the matter Can't we come, or. I don't wonder why. Let's go. Where. Where is our home again. I will not go to your house today. I will go one day later. Today I went out with him a little. All right. Then I go. Jas will have to travel one day. Let's go. Nila also loved Nahid very much at one time. Later found out, that there is a relationship with Rina. So he did not express his love. The fair has been well organized. He looked around for a long time. Fuchka, jillipi khelo dujane. Bought two thefts. Rina K. Rina is very happy getting two stolen. Rina said after walking around. Now I have to go home. You're going home, Then let's go. You stand for a while. I bring a bicycle. Rina got on the bicycle again. He came down to the mango orchard. Nahid said let's go a little further. The jungle. You can give it. At that time Rina is looking at Nahid's lips. What's the matter, why are you looking at me like this. I don't feel ashamed. No, I don't think so. What a shame for me. You are all mine. I gave you everything I had. When Rina looked at him, she hugged and kissed Nahid. Nahid himself does not know. Nahid got excited and started kissing him too. Put your hands on the scalp and hair. Great time. What an intimate relationship. The kissing process lasted for about five minutes. Then it stopped. This time Rina is very happy. And with that came shame. Looking down. Nahid raised her chin with her hand and said, No more getting embarrassed. My bride is my wife. Now go home. And be careful. Go home and massage. I'll go when you get home. You go i can go Rina crossed the pond again and entered her house through the window of the house. And massaging Nahid K. She has reached home. Nahid calmly left for his home.

(5)

The results of the test will be announced on Monday. The school authorities will send the high school to the board only if they pass the test from the school. So both of them went that day to know the result of the test. Rina and Nahid are both good students. So it will give good results. He has faith in them. All students are waiting for notice. That is when the head teacher will get the result out. In the end, at eleven forty minutes, Peon result was killed on the notice board. Everyone rushed to see the result. Lots of crowds now. You will see when the crowd decreases. Within half an hour the crowd had subsided. Rina and Nahid went to see the result. Both have passed. Good number. But Rina's number has decreased a lot. He has reduced his reading this time. However, Nahid scolded him several times. Nahid asked Rina to read with her mind. Go home and play a few bushes. To Ramadan Matabbar. I thought you would brighten the face of the village. But if you do such a result, my value will be respected. The next three months Will read well. And I will tell Fazal Mia from tomorrow. You can read to him. Fazal Mia is not as good as the master. Rina says I will not go to study with her father. He is a different person. Bad eyes. You have to go to Fazal Mia. Rina doesn't want to go for another reason. Reading at night. Moreover, badass Sujan fell there. Who knows what will happen. So he is scared. But Riner does not have the courage to tell his father. So the next day I am going to study at Mr. Fazal's house. In the evening. Winter time. Dark. Of course there is a torch in hand. I have to go a lot. It will be about half a kilometer. Small forests in places. Again there is a little space. Settle somewhere again. What else happens in the village. Privately with Sujan every day. Now Sujan is very happy. Because, It would be great to impress Rina. One day he said. Well, I'll take Rina. I love you so much. I want to get married. Will you marry me Yes i agree If you can give me endless love. I can. Yes, I can. True. Okay, then what can I do for you. Take a look at what to do. If I say, I have to get rid of the irritation of my body here today. I can. Sujan says to herself, how long? Every day I talk hot. Not in love. I know beautiful girls. What do they love for? What are you thinking? Can't spend an hour with me today. Why can't I, I am a traveler on that path. You don't know Nahid will never give this to you. Listen, I know you. What a boy you are. Guys like you think nothing but dirty talk. You said a good thing. Nahid will not give me these. I know how great he is. That's why I love him. And I don't want friends like you. And I am not coming privately from tomorrow. All right, don't come. Today that makes me happy. Saying this, he grabbed Rina by the side of the road. Falls on the grass. Rolling on the grass. They both deal with their confidence as they choose to embark on their play activities. Rina tries her best to save herself. But it continues to fail. A few times on the breast, I was going to put my hand in my mouth. The clothes tear a bit. At that time Nahid reached like an angel. Nahid grabbed Sujan's collar and started beating her. Hit the nose. Blood is gurgling. Sujan is no longer able to. He runs. Rina started crying loudly. What happened to me? Nahid, I can't show you my face. What's wrong, let's go home. Today I come to your house. Now there is no one on the street. He took Rina home. There was no Ramadan Matabbar at home. No one could find out. Only mother knew. Mother gives a lot of peace. Nahid will stay in Rina's house for an hour. Will explain. Rina came home after the dress. The door slammed shut. Forget what happened Rina. Think nothing happened to you. I'm here. I never misunderstood you. I still don't understand. You will not do any madness. Auntie, Aunt mother. What happened, Dad? There is rice. There is Dad. Bring it. I'll feed you. Here Rina's mother realizes that Nahid has a relationship with Rina. He goes to fetch food without saying anything, and thinks Nahid is a good boy. It would be good if they had a relationship. But on the other hand, it would be a disaster, if Rina's father knew, he would not keep them. Bring food. This is not Dad. See what to eat. Well, Dad, let me tell you something. What are you talking about, aunt? Doesn't mean you two love each other? After a while, he died. Then Rina's mother says that my father has no problem with me. Take care of your uncle and brother. Otherwise there is danger again. No aunt nothing will happen. Bless us. Nahid mixes a little rice. Riner put it in his mouth. After feeding a few times. Rina plays with her own hands. Nahid put his hand on Rina's head and came home calmly. Nahid can't sleep all night. Epas opas. The night does not cut. He just thinks, That Sujan will not leave if given a chance. Hit his heart. One day or another will take revenge.

(2)

Sadeq Ali, a dear friend of Ramadan. Everyone calls him Sadeq. He is as cunning but educated as Ramadan. Another madman of the society. The boys are educated. Some are doctors, some are masters. Youngest son Asik Ali. He has been mastering for some time. Got it in the village school. Primary school teacher. He is also getting good salary. Looking for a bride for the wedding. The blessing of the neighborhood said, the bride is in our house uncle. Niyamat is Sadeq Ali's work man. Sadeq's peers. Has grown from small to large at the same time. Like a friend Who is the blessing? Hey uncle is our Ramadan little girl. That's right. Absolutely forgot to kill. The girl is good, Good looking. He is also very good at studying. All right, Asik will marry Ramzan's daughter. I will tell Ramadan tomorrow. Well, what happened to Niyamat Karim's land? Has the land agreed to survive? No, uncle. Karim people know differently. How mad. Who is turning the society around without getting mad. Or people are going to him now. Some people are hanging out with him. You know the blessing, the man is good. But if people are given good intellect in this way, my kingdom will not last after a while. Panchayat vote in front. Keep a cool head.

A few days later, Sadeq Ali met Ramzan. What's the matter Mia. This time there is no Parthi in your booth. Who has the courage to fight against me? He is. There is some fear in my booth. Who is that guy Karim? Yes brother Ramadan. Talk about rubbing salt in my wounds - d'oh! Will not delay the marriage of the daughter. I have to pay. It has grown. So I was saying that I got my Asik mastery. So I was saying that I would not have got married. But the word is not bad, Sadeq. That would be nice. Now keep talking. I will discuss later. Look, I'm talking about being the father of the boy. I'm thinking. All right, Sadeq will marry your son. I promised this. Sitting on the field. I will go to your house tomorrow, Sadeq. We have to sit somewhere. Although not a party, I will sit in the discussion as the head of the village. You go now. Sadeq Matabbar educated, But also intriguing. Many lands of Matabbar of Ramadan. About two hundred bighas. One son and one daughter. Owns huge assets. Ramadan is not educated but the captain of the two booths. Society is in his hands. Ramzan lies in bed at home at night and tells Ginny, you know Rina's mother. I met Sadeq in the garden this afternoon. That's what happened. No. Nothing like that happened. Rina was talking about marriage. What are you talking about? Rina's marriage to the youngest son of Sadeq Matabbar of that neighborhood. Of course, the proposal belongs to Sadeq. I say leave it at that. Why leave it out, you don't have to get married. Have to pay. You have to look for a good boy, you have to look for five places. And besides, there is the matter of Rina's opinion. So no. That's it. Matabbar said, we have to get married in the village. I have a daughter. Don't give it, we'll be fine. It is good to see Karim's son in the village. Yeah Al that sounds pretty crap to me, Looks like BT aint for me either. But boy Karim gives knowledge to the society. That's why I don't like it. I'm crazy, What will happen to me if people follow his knowledge. There will be honor. Let's see. That's why I'm not giving my daughter to Sadeq's house. O Shala has made this proposal to grab my land. In that case, I will marry Karim's son. I'll tell you something. Tell me what to say. Guys, there is a relationship between them. They both love each other. I didn't know he was. I know. Then there was no problem. All right, sleep. Ramadan began to fall asleep. Ramadan is politically cunning but not cunning with boys and girls. Knows to give the dignity of love. Because he was married to Rina's mother. He has a great story. I know. Then there was no problem. All right, sleep. Ramadan began to fall asleep. Ramadan is politically cunning but not cunning with boys and girls. Knows to give the dignity of love. Because he was married to Rina's mother. He has a great story. I know. Then there was no problem. All right, sleep. Ramadan began to fall asleep. Ramadan is politically cunning but not cunning with boys and girls. Knows to give the dignity of love. Because he was married to Rina's mother. He has a great story.

(2)

And a few days are left out of the high school examination. Extremely stressful study. Both are stepping up. Rina has dropped out of Fazal Master. Rina comes to teach Ritu Madam. At Rina's house. Rina's mother fixed it. At that time, Rina's mobile phone rang. There was a ringtone, he said favorite and favorite ... Dad can't catch because he's in front. The phone rang a few times. Barren again. That's when Rina's father said. Rina ... hold my mother's phone. He took the phone and came inside the room. Hello, now there's Dad. I'll call later. Ramzan Ali suddenly enters Rina's room. Rina was scared. Ramadan asks, What the heck mom. Who were you talking to? Rina is scared. The eyes were twinkling. The darling daughter of Ramadan. Never killed. He never even gave a threat. But everyone is scared to see his character. In that case, Rina also gets. His last words in the village. Tell me, mother. Rina can't tell. Ramzan sits next to Rina, the girl, and shakes her head. I'm scared. I'm not as bad as you are, mother. You were talking to Nahid. Rina was terrified when she heard Nahid's words from her father's mouth. Scared. Do you love Nahid? Don't say anything. Mother Ray, I know everything, your mother told me everything. I will marry you to Nahid. I promise. Really dad. Yes mother yes. Rina hugs her father. Dad we're so scared of you, but you're really good. Ok All right mom. Ask Nahid to come home tomorrow. And pay attention to both of them during the exam. There is a lot of time to tell stories. Panchayat elections are ahead again. I have a lot of work to do. Dad, I have to give you a word. Tell me. You will not do dirty work and politics in the society. Many people call you bad. I do not like to hear. No, mother, don't tell me that. I can't keep this in your life. Not even God Himself. Why Dad why. Everyone sees my outside and no one sees my inside. So call me a lot worse. You will invite Nahid tomorrow. We will eat together at home at night. How? All right, Dad. All right. No. So call me a lot worse. You will invite Nahid tomorrow. We will eat together at home at night. How? All right, Dad. All right. No. So call me a lot worse. You will invite Nahid tomorrow. We will eat together at home at night. How? All right, Dad. All right.

The next morning, it will be exactly eight o'clock. He came to Rina's house. Mr. Moral. Mr. Moral. Are you at home? Who am I? I am Niyamat, uncle. Come and bless. So Mr. Sadeq is fine. Yes, it is good, but in a big way. Why. Nothing like that is a big thought again. Hey, well done. Looking to get married for our master. But not matching anyone. Yes, the day before yesterday he was telling me in the garden. Yes. Uncle went home and said. That's the kind of thing that comes up. Oh. So sit down. That's good. I also agreed to give. True. Yes Ray. Rina was at home, heard. He is devastated. Dad then lied to me. She can't think anymore. Hey that blessing, I will tell Sadeq that marriage cannot be given before the election. All right uncle, then I will get up now. All right, come on. After Niyamat left, Ramzan said, Shala has brought marriage to my house. Rina's mother, you're listening. I will never marry Sadeq's house. You bastards, What if there is an educated family. Damn big bastard. Rina's mother let me eat something. There is a meeting in that neighborhood today. It is a matter of election. Everyone in the neighborhood is listening to Karim. Sadeq will not be able to win the election this time. Lots of trouble. Last time Sadeq Mastani won. However, his name was not made public. The thugs were brought from outside. This time most of the people do not want Sadeq. Who knows who will be our party member this time. That is the matter of the region president. There will be no party in my booth. I told you. And if he gives, what will he do? What else should I do, he has to see. I have won without voting all my life, this time I will win. Anyway. Give me food. Giving, Wash your hands and face. Ramzan Matabbar refreshed himself and came to the dinner table. Sit down and play Ramadan Matabbar Bhimri. Because today Sadh has young goat meat. She is happy to see. Saliva is dripping from the tongue. Wife, what's the matter today, you cooked goat meat. You can't see goat meat. Cook it again. Thank you for what your wife says. No, not at all. Now eat. Your daughter has come, she says she will feed you. Rina brings it for me. Yes, he cooked it. Is that so? Besides, who called Nahid today. Oh so. What he said. She doesn't want to come. Because you are very scared. Oh that's good It is better to be afraid. Everyone in the village is afraid of me. Power is needed. I want to be strict and temperamental to run the society. Otherwise it is not. But you also have to be humble. But many people call you insidious. Let him do it. I have no interest in seeing him. Take this meat. Hey, don't give up. I have eaten a lot. Another one. This is the bone of the chest. Give when you say. Yes my mom cooked. Where is he? Dako will not eat. Eat. Eat later. Went to the rock house. What notes or photos to bring. Dad said to actually eat. Yes, will you marry Nahid? You have to think. If they both like it, then you have to pay. Exclude those things, when it will happen. I got up. Will you go somewhere now? Yes, I will. There is a meeting in that neighborhood. If I don't go, I won't sit in the discussion again. Go. I said come back in the evening. Why. Who called Nahid. Oh. All right. I will leave. When it will happen. I got up. Will you go somewhere now? Yes, I will. There is a meeting in that neighborhood. If I don't go, I won't sit in the discussion again. Go. I said come back in the evening. Why. Who called Nahid. Oh. All right. I will leave. When it will happen. I got up. Will you go somewhere now? Yes, I will. There is a meeting in that neighborhood. If I don't go, I won't sit in the discussion again. Go. I said come back in the evening. Why. Who called Nahid. Oh. All right. I will leave. When it will happen. I got up. Will you go somewhere now? Yes, I will. There is a meeting in that neighborhood. If I don't go, I won't sit in the discussion again. Go. I said come back in the evening. Why. Who called Nahid. Oh. All right. I will leave. When it will happen. I got up. Will you go somewhere now? Yes, I will. There is a meeting in that neighborhood. If I don't go, I won't sit in the discussion again. Go. I said come back in the evening. Why. Who called Nahid. Oh. All right. I will leave.

8

Today is the political program in the tenth parliament. Organized by People's Party of Thamathampur. That is the meeting of the party of Ramadan. Ramzan Matabbar is the special guest. Many leaders and dignitaries present at the discussion meeting. But leaders and activists are waiting for Ramadan. Meanwhile, Nahid has promised Rina K. They will go home today. But Mr. Matabbar is very scared. So there is a lot of fear. But he thought that he was the one who told me to go, said Rina. But tell me something. He came out almost in the afternoon. He was walking. Thin creeper of the forest tree in hand. Turning his hand and coming to sing. The song was "I am Tore Baisa. I have a good mind. Baisa is good. Meanwhile, Ramzan Matabbar attended the meeting. But where are the people. It is empty. Only the leaders and workers. And a few usurers are sitting. To listen to the discussion of Ramadan. . Hare Niazaddi. Where are the people? Mr. Moral is not there from the beginning. What is he? All right, cancel the meeting. To be canceled. Yes canceled. Local meeting will be held tomorrow. The party will be in the office. The letter will be sent. Niazddi I went home.

Nahid is standing in the mango orchard. Wondering if you can. If you do something, uncle Ramzan. On the other hand, he thinks that Rina will tell me then. Not so. Whatever is in the forehead. Or I gave my life for love. I'll remember. Going to think. Meet Sujan at that time. Sujan bows her head and tries to escape. That shit shit. That's it. Sujan started running without looking back. Eventually Sujan escaped. Nahid is very excited. Why not hapapei. Talk about revenge. I left for a couple of minutes and sat down. This time he got up again and walked along the road. Rina's house in front. Big house. The best house in the village. Speaking of the zamindar's house. About two hundred bighas of land for Ramadan. Nahid walked inside the house. Rina's mother was seen. Aunt mother Rina is not there. There is in his house. No problem to go. Rina and Rina's mother. Nahid has arrived. Take it. Rina came down from the second floor smiling happily. Rina said, I couldn't think, You will come Go to Baba Rina's house. Nahid climbed the stairs. Inside the house. There are stairs to go up to the second floor. It's a big deal. What they can't do. Clean house. Decorated with valuable things. A few days ago, Rina's house was on the ground floor. Now upstairs. Nahid went to Rina's house and was surprised. So nicely decorated house. Foreign furniture. Even the sitting sofa. Hey what are you thinking Sit down, I'll bring you some coffee. Oh no no. No need to bring. Sit down and talk. Nahid said as if you are feeling new today. I feel like I'm with a stranger. Why. Not just like that. I will say one thing Rina. Tell me. Well tell me why I was called today. I do not know. Dad said to call I called diameter. I don't know anything else. You sit down and I'll get you some coffee. The people of Kofi village do not know that. I don't understand. But the rich talk about home. Rina's house is always available. Rina came down. At that time Ramadan Matabbar also entered. To mutter. Dad, you should be in the meeting now. Suddenly at home. Don't say anymore. There are no people in the meeting. Who will be the meeting. I will choose the party with whom. That is our business. You don't have to understand. Dad. What to say. Yes, Dad. Tell me. Guys Nahid has arrived. Oh well. So where is that gentleman. Upstairs Sitting in my room. You gave me something to eat. No, Dad. All right, bring some coffee. I'm in your room Going. Oh yes don't forget to bring it for me. All right, Dad. Can I forget you? All right, go. Rina's mother, oh Rina's mother. Listen. Say yes The baby was not supposed to come today. Yes. He informed by phone that he will not go home in next one week. There is still work to be done. Oh. So Nahid has come. Yes. Did you talk? No such thing was said. Ok i'm going I will not go. You go All right. Mr. Ramzan went to the door of Rina's house and shook his head. Huh huh. Somehow it doesn't come in my language. Hey uncle. How are you Good. How are you Everyone in the house is fine. Yes uncle. Nahid was silent for a while. No talking. Dumb. Matabbar said, Is your father misleading people? No, uncle. My father is a very different person. He wants people well. Never want bad. Rina appeared to talk like that. A glass of coffee in hand. With some foreign chanachur. Matabbar loves to eat chanachur with coffee. This is Daddy Coffee and your Chanachur. Hey, give it to Nahid first. No, you take it first. Matabbar said with a sip of coffee. Look, father Nahid. I know about you. Your aunt said. I have no objection to that. But the leaders do not like your father. Maybe one day you will hear that your father has been taken to the police. Explain to your father. Don't get involved in politics. Not everyone has to do everything if they know how to study. Uncle, it is better for my father to say these things. I don't want to get involved. I student people do not understand all that. Sadeq is also insisting on your father's land. Everything comes to my ears, father. Then Rina said, Dad, what are you saying to him? Don't drag him into Osbe. Where am I pulling, what else have I said? All right, you guys. I wake up. How to eat together at night. Then how to go home. No, I have to go home, uncle. Talk to you soon and keep up the good content.

9

Rina came after it in a beautiful dress. What a beautiful dress. Very clean. Like a beautiful princess. That will see. He must be in love with Rina. But now Rina wants to tell me something. Not something else. I do not understand the matter at all. Pink lipstick on the lips. There is a fierce hunger in the eyes. Light stomach is out. The waist is visible. The saree is georgette pink. Pink bangle in hand. It is quite understandable that this is the bangle I bought. I bought it at the fair in Boxiganj. He is quite agreeable. At that moment Rina said, "Are you not dreaming, Mr. Wake up?" Oh no I mean yes. What? What do you really think? I will say. Don't hit. Seeing you today, I think it is not a princess seen in a dream, but a princess seen in reality. And you thought, You think I'm excited about something. The aggression that is hiding inside your mind is coming. Did you find me as stupid as the other girls? Wait, it's yours. Saying this, Rina pushed Nahid to the bed. And sat on his chest. This is what you are doing. Anyone can leave. Let him come. Is your day my day? Both of them spread their arms. Rina says look at me like other girls. Hey what did I say. I have said what your mind has said. What is my fault in this? I don't know that. Bear with me as you have told me. What will you do No, I won't do anything. I will do what you say. Chu .... mu ...... khab. But you are insisting Rina. I'll do it a hundred times. You can stop. No, I don't want that. Sujan told me exactly that day. What did he say? Said that Nahid will never be able to give you anything. Rather I will get everything. Yes, you stay with him. I don't need I don't want that now. We have to study and grow up. I went. Be well Listen Nahid. No, I don't want to hear anything from you. Nahid hurried down to the ground floor. And he left the house to greet Ramzan Matabbar. Rina stood on the second floor in surprise and anger. He never thought. It will happen. However, Rinar is also less hot. If you say love, you have to do a lot of things. There is nothing wrong with that. Love is a symbol of beauty. I don't think there is anything wrong with that. He's a little too honest. Not so honest. What kind of love if you can't give a little satisfaction to your lover. Or by love or what gain. Who will understand him. But it is true that, The boy is not greedy. Gentle enough. But I need to be a little different. No no I don't know what he thinks. He came down to the lower room muttering to himself.

Chapter 2

There is no meeting of Matabbar in the party office today. Yes brother Fazlu. Won't you go? If you go, you will hear something. But whatever I say, Niaz. But the post of secretary is not right at all now. Why brother Fazlu. Hey Mia, you've been at the party for about ten to fifteen years. Yes, I am. But look, you have the same position. You can't be president or party. It's a team matter. But Niaz can do everything in Ramadan. I heard Parthi is not getting it. So don't look at who says Ramadan. What to say. What can I say? Hey, as an asshole, we don't think badly of you. If not, what is the benefit of the team. Sagir Mia became a member after you. I will not let him stand this time. See what he is saying. After a while all the team members and staff appeared. Now Ramadan is waiting for Matabbar. He also does not know when the leader will come. Ahmed says where is Niaz, At least give me tea biscuits. Hey Matabbar, let's go. It's not clear when that guy will come. One by one, everyone in the group said, so let's have tea before he comes. What are you all right. Some people said yes, yes, so be it. Niaz is in trouble. Will be the party secretary. But Mr. Matabbar treats him like the LCS of the party. Hey Matabbar Mister is coming. It came. Why didn't Niazaddi give them tea? This is going. So tell me how you are. I'm fine Moral Mister. Everyone said at once. So what do you think, who can be parthi. Rahim and Nader whispered an agreement. Then it was said that our nominated candidate is Bakul Master. What do you say? Yes, the man is not bad, of course. Speaking of the master. Will he do politics. He will be seen either. Matabbar says, Or I will finally make Karim stand. What's up. Then tomorrow Rahim and Nader's brothers go to Bakul. This time we have to win anyway. Once again with Sadeq Gunda

Won not this time. Fazlu then said, he was done for you. No need to worry. Talk about rubbing salt in my wounds - d'oh! Talk to you soon and keep up the good content. You're talking too much. Do you understand politics? Nowadays I can hear you misunderstanding him. Listen, I'll be more mad, I'll cut off my leg. No father can save. Where is Fazil? Who called you here? Where is Fazil? Fazlu grumbled and left. We have to form a committee in a new way. They can do all that to win votes. Otherwise, the region president will not have the value. Then tomorrow, Rahim and Nader's brothers, come to Bakul Master's house. I'm leaving Ray Niaz. I have some work to do in my booth.

11

Fazlu goes to the house of Sheikh Karim i.e. Nahid. Brother Karim, are you at home? Yes i am Income. What's the matter, Ray? Everyone is fine at home. Yeah Al that sounds pretty crap to me, Looks like BT aint for me either. This is Nahid's mother listening. Say yes Do not give two cups of tea. Giving. Hey, what's the matter, Fazlu Deora. What's the matter No, I came to talk to this big brother. Oh, you guys tell the story. I bring tea. Yeah Al that sounds pretty crap to me, Looks like BT aint for me either. No, I don't have to praise anymore. It's been a long time.

Yes, what did you say? I am telling you to become a party member in the election. What do you say? These will not be done by me. Why not. Hey, it is not possible for everyone to do politics. The people of the village are by your side. Even if it is or what. There are many people to do politics. I give good advice to people, that's enough. The party of Ramadan has decided to field Bakul Master. So I understand. Good on the one hand. Master people know all the laws. Big brother, you are no less. Even if you are not well educated, everyone knows your knowledge. You move away. What bit you mad dog. No, brother, I was not bitten by a mad dog. I will not leave that guy Ramadan. Sala insults me, Among the people. The rich say they all agree. No more. This time I will choose the best person. If I need to, I have thirty bighas of land and I want to sell it and lose Sala. Hey, did you really bite the mad dog? Listen, brother, you have to stand up. I will call a few good people and form a committee myself. I will not let them loot anymore. This time you are right. That's supposed to be a committee with good people. So see if it is. Then I am willing to enter politics. Besides, people like Sadeq no longer have the ability to win in this booth. All right, let's arrange a meeting at my house. All right. I'm leaving, brother. Hey, don't drink tea. No, stay today. No time. I will come and eat later. Nahid comes and says, Father, you become a party in the election. Stand by the good people of the village. Show me who the right leader is. He can be done. But we don't have property, father. No money. It takes a lot of money to fight them. Need a young boy. But the people in the area like you very much. Nahid's mother Rangila came and said, "Hey, where did Deora go?" He is gone. He said he would eat tea. Eat his food instead. Nahid you take. I have All right. Nahid's mother went inside. Nahis said with a sip of tea, Well, father, did you tell Sadeq to sell that land? Impossible. I will never sell that land. I have only ten bighas of land so that your future can be cut well. And those two bighas are my father's land. I will not live even if I die. Father's blessings are in him. Sadeq or what I want to buy to straighten the stain. Yes, I heard. He wants to buy by force. If you insist. There is no law court in the country. There is just justice. Besides, I don't have to worry about that. If I don't give them my land, they have nothing to do. Niyamat came a few days ago to talk about land. I made it clear. All right, you don't have to think about that. Basga to read. Going. But think of Fazlur, father.

12

Nahid and Rina have not been in touch for several days. Of course, Rina called several times. But Nahid did not receive the call. School is also a holiday. Private vacation. No friend now communicates with anyone like that. Because the pressure of examination is on everyone's head. That he is not stressed. Absolutely a matter of honor. He can either eat the bush with his parents. But girls have to live with their heads held high. And especially to Promika. But Nahid is not afraid of Osbe. Who is Nahid's only fear? She wants to read. I want a good job. Much more. Nahid entered his room after drinking tea. To read. Open the south window. A light breeze is blowing through the windows. Feeling mildly cold. Lots of books arranged on the table. He is flipping through the pages of the chemistry book. Again, you know, the hall was closed. No, it doesn't feel good. The mind does not feel calm. Walking. Sat down again. The bed was remote. TV with remote ' Turned on. Sony entered eight channels. Nahid is thinking what to see. With this Gopal started watching cartoons of clowns. Watching for a while, suddenly a message came on the mobile. As soon as you click on the message, the texts start flashing. Beloved, I have been calling you for the last three years. You are not receiving the phone without being kind to me. I want to see you at least one last time. Please come to our mango orchard tomorrow. I'll be waiting for you. If not here's a new product just for you! I have been calling you for the last three years. You are not receiving the phone without being kind to me. I want to see you at least one last time. Please come to our mango orchard tomorrow. I'll be waiting for you. If not here's a new product just for you! I have been calling you for the last three years. You are not receiving the phone without being kind to me. I want to see you at least one last time. Please come to our mango orchard tomorrow. I'll be waiting for you. If not here's a new product just for you!

After reading the message, he replied without thinking of anything. I don't have to talk to any rude girl. He can do whatever you want. I love you but I'm not Sujan. You compared Sujan to me. You know better, I don't like it. I love but I don't want illicit intercourse. When did you kiss that day? Yet I said nothing. You attacked again. I'm not like that at all. Diameter reply is over. There was no reply from either side. Nahid studies a lot. The suffering of love is not less. Still, he is studying by ignoring the suffering. Check ahead. You have to get good results. I want to be a big officer when I grow up. On the other hand, some villagers are upset about my father's politics. Especially Fazlu Sheikh. His party will form a panchayat as much as it costs.

13

Sadeq Matabbar is deeply concerned about the way the storm of politics is raging in the village and it is becoming impossible for him to do politics. The last panchayat won by hooliganism because of their party. Now that too is out of hand. Ramzan's party has formed a panchayat. As a result, there will be no official jury of Sadeq. The police will catch him. Earlier Ramzan and Sadeq Saheb used to form panchayats. Either Ramzan's team or Sadeq's team. Now both parties are going to be proletarians. The only reason is Karim. That guy is stepping on their ripe paddy.

Rahim and Nader Bakul explained a lot to Master. To fight him in the election. But Bakul did not master. That said, I teach master students. Not politics for me. Rather I am against politics. He further said that I am supporting you, there is no problem in voting. But don't tell me that. Rahim and Nader have been trying to explain for the last two days. But all their efforts have failed. The election is coming up. Thamathampur panchayat has only five seats. There have been three gram panchayats. He has two seats in Thamathampur. There are parliaments number one and two. A few days ago, the panchayat was divided and separated. It happened before the election. At that time Thamathampur was the tenth and eleventh parliament. Now the fully independent panchayat is in Thamathampur. Rahim and Nader come to Ramzan Matabbar's house. The three of them decide together, Who will stand for Nader? The announcement of the diameter of the party last Ramadan. In the evening there will be a meeting with the team members. For the new party. Nader said the new party means. Our party will be formed separately. I went to the head office yesterday. The president of the region has been in trouble with me. I have come to say on the face. I left the party. Mr. Moral, it was not right. Everyone knows the old party. It could have been changed later. Even if you don't think about it. It is my responsibility to pass. Don't let their party win here. We will join Sadeq if needed. There will be alliance parties. The panchayat will be ours. Can We will join Sadeq if needed. There will be alliance parties. The panchayat will be ours. Can We will join Sadeq if needed. There will be alliance parties. The panchayat will be ours.

14

The next morning, Fazlu and three others came to Karim's house. Big brother, I have come to you. You will not return to me today. With three wise men came. Karim said, "Hey, what are you doing?" Exclude acts of violence. Not politics for us. Politics is for the rich. Big brother, you don't have to worry about that. I'll take a look at them. You agree once. This is what I have brought with Bakul Master, Khalek Bhai and Nifaz Doctor. We need good people in our region. So at least you have to do the politics. Bakul Master says, listen big brother I am not speaking as Master Speaking as a younger brother. You agree. In unison, Khaleq and Nifaz said, Brother, agree. We are educated people. We want to educate this barbaric society. We are with you Rahim and Nader went to this Bakul Bhai to join their party. The master could have agreed but did not. Yet politics will do with us. We are all new brothers. I don't see that success can come once. Everyone in the five booths is staring you in the face. Waiting for you Big brother, if you are a candidate in the election, you will definitely get at least four seats. Nahid's mother comes with tea. Well, Bapu, don't agree when everyone is saying. Most of the people in the village want you. Mr. Karim has been sitting in silence for a long time. Ekdam th mare. Then comes the answer. I agree. But you have to be with me all the time. You have to give the right advice. Tell me if you can. I agree. Fazlu Sheikh said. Yes. One hundred. Then come to my house this afternoon. With two dozen more. To general meeting. Just talk. There is a need to exchange views with everyone. Fazlu nodded. At that time Nahid came out of the house. Dad is sitting in the yard. Nahid is riding a bicycle somewhere. Dad says, Where are you going now dad. No dad has a little work out there. Will be back soon. Must stay in the afternoon. There is some work to be done at home. All right, Dad said, got on the bike and walked on the red road. On the edge of the mango orchard. Something has to go. From here to there. Rina is waiting for Nahid. It was supposed to come at night. But after that the time has been changed by massaging. Cycling Slowly, of course. Canceled the old bike. He took a new bicycle to his father. Ladies bicycle. Gearing system. There are five gears. Good kind of money has been spent. About five thousand. The road is left in front of Mithuta. Wondering what to say. If he doesn't like me on the bus then I'm done. I will not live without Rina. Oh god you save me I don't want anything bad either. But I also needed to think about the other side. A little bit of romance. I don't want anything else. I don't see any fault in him. But who knows what ghost was in his head. Or holding hands and apologizing I'll take it. Slowly cycling but still hopping. It is throbbing inside the chest. What will happen. Who knows Meet Aziz on the street. Aziz is a friend of Nahid. Where are you going now? No, there's a little work here. No, You look worried. Why are you laughing No, no. Where are you? Hey guy, looking at you, it looks like you are hapless. Tell me what's the matter. I don't know what to say. There is nothing to say. I mean there. And you don't have to mean it. Tell me the matter. If not, I went. I mean, my relationship with Rina is fading, Ray. He used to say what can be done. What kind I haven't spoken for a week for a word. I was very angry. Tangled up. Oh this thing. And no matter what. Go yourself and say sorry to him. Do whatever you want. Do as he pleases. Hey, that's what happens when you make love, boy. Didn't see what happened to my one month with Oliver. Who else gave it with the mind. Hey girls are roses. If you want to keep that rose, you have to take care of it. I don't do much to keep the rose alive. Yes. So do that. Keep it the way you want it to be. Then you will see that the rose means Rina will be yours. Well, brother, you have a little time Don't explain it to him. Well, I'll say okay. I have a good relationship with you. That's right. Saying this, he put a paw on Nahid's back. And gave confidence. Nahid rode his bicycle. Nayanader entered the house. Aren't you looking? I'm here, I'm here. What news. Aren't you studying? Yes, he said yes. Check ahead. Well, I'm listening to whether your father will contest the election. Yes. Dad was not agreeing. Then Fazlu uncle, Bakul Sir Khaled uncle has persuaded many more. That's good. Abba also said that if Nahid's father contests the election this time, no one will get a seat. Leaders are so optimistic. The people of the village are getting the right leader this time. Everyone deserves to improve. Exclude all that. Listen to me. I will say something. I have come to say yes. If not, what have I come to do in the afternoon? Hey, it's three o'clock in the afternoon. Oh this is your knowledge. Even if it is three o'clock, it is not in the afternoon. Yes afternoon but start in the afternoon. Whatever he is. I have to go somewhere. Where. In Rina's mango orchard. Why, don't fall in love with me. Ah, What nonsense are you talking about? My pet month is going on. And you're joking. Where did I make jokes. It's not funny. I don't understand the meaning of taking me to the garden. What do you want to do? Nayana turned her face to the other side and smiled. He turned his face again. I don't know if today's boys have faith. All greedy. Dhyut Tarika says Nahid is going to come straight out of the house. At that time, Nayana grabbed the collar of the shirt from behind and said, I made up my mind. But I told you to be angry. Tell me what you mean. What more can I say. You are saying the opposite. Hey, you are our best friend. We all love you I also like. Then there is no right to fan. Yes, but not all the time. All right, tell me. Rina said she would come to the garden. After dusk but he says to come again in the afternoon. I haven't spoken to him in three days. There is anger. Sometimes it can leave me. My Saturn phase is going on. Oh this thing. So why go to their house in the garden. I can't go to the garden. Why. You have no commons sense. The two of them in the garden in the afternoon. What do people say you have a passion. What can be done then. Huh let me think. Feelings. The idea is to do one thing. What. I mean, I call Rina. Let me settle the matter. All right. Say it. But on what pretext will I go? What an excuse to ask for notes again. Oh good idea. But will he agree? I see the point in agreeing. That's right There is a mobile phone. Not from my mobile. Do it with your mobile. All right. Bring the mobile. There is that room. I will open the window. Give. It would be nice to have air. Nayana pushes and opens. And goes to bring mobile in another room. Came with mobile. Rina K called. Kring Kring Kring did for a while. Received the phone. Hello Rina. No, I'm Rina's mother. Assalamu Alaikum Khalamma. I'm not. What is she, mother? Say something. Yes aunt. Who needs Rina? All right. Rina Rina mother. Aren't you What happened? Why are you shouting? This is what Nayana called. See what you have to say. Oh give it. Don't talk I go and see what happens to the food. I have finished work again. I was born in a big house. I came to work in a big house. Half no dad. Rina picks up the phone and says, What's the matter? No searches. You have completely disappeared. No, now you can understand the pressure of studying. I leave out all that. That's why I called. Well, one more thing. What is the news of your Nahid? And the news. That's crazy. You're crazy. I was in love with a madman at one time, what happened again. Didn't breakup Marley. Why should I break the bastard breakup? One is crazy. Something works like crazy. Then you don't want to get involved in the relationship. Hey, tell me what to say. Show ... no I'm not crazy. But the guy drove me crazy. Can I live without that crazy person? Impossible. As long as I have life, I will fall in love with the madman. There was a problem in the middle. Shala wanted to kiss. But Shala didn't pay attention to me. There is some anger for this. I thought again. No, it's my fault. As beautiful as she looks, she is also beautiful inside the mind. So your anger has subsided. I was angry for a few hours. Then don't do it anymore. That's right, This is not right before marriage. Moreover, father and mother have also agreed to get married. What I say is true. So what does it mean to do so. Hey, I let him get a little hurt. Understand the true meaning of love. Nahid was listening. We were talking on loudspeakers. But I was scared yesterday. In the garden. I said come on, I don't really love that anymore. Really. Hey shit no ray. You don't even understand being my girlfriend. How to understand. Nahid is very happy. He said, you want me to be happy by suffering. Hey you are here Yes i'm here Nayana, you cheated with me. I came home crying. You're in the garden. You called, so take me with you. So that's what I mean for you. Oh. I understand that the prince has suffered a lot. Ore babu shona. Don't get angry, don't get angry. All right, then do one thing. After dusk. Come to our house, you two will talk. And Nahid. Hey, I'm asking you to come with Nahid. All right. I'm keeping. Yes. After talking on the phone, Nayana said to Nahid, Listen, I understand that there is nothing wrong with him. It's your fault. He loves you so much that he will never give himself up again. And your wit, I can't satisfy my lover's little whims right now. It doesn't matter now. Increases more love in these. Love makes you fresh. Feel a little serious. How? Which will go after dusk. Don't buy another rose. Let's go. If you can, eat a few puffs. All right, get ready in the evening, I'll be on time. All right.

15

Khalik and Nifaz doctors have gathered hundreds of people. There are a lot of young boys among them. They are like masters to be used as an army. The team program will be made in Karim's new home. There are older people. With young men. They will run the team. They need to keep the society healthy and strong. Fazlu Sheikh is not sitting on it in anger. He is entering politics to make the society better. But he is the main person of the team. But he fought this election for the sake of the people. Niyamat came and informed Sadeq Matabbar who. Hundreds of people are said to have come to Karim's uncle's house. When. In the evening. Oh. Where did you hear that? Fazlu Sheikh was talking in that Bazlur tea shop. The panda of that group. Uncle was saying why Fazlu Ebuth will get at least three or four seats. How do I understand? Everyone in this village supports Karim. Niyamat politics you do not understand so much. Parthi see as much as they can. No problem. I will win the vote. What does. Hey, the people of the village get a couple of rupees Sit crouched. Let them play khala. When the time comes, I will win. I'm listening too. What an uncle. I hear his field is very good. Excluding his own booth, he is doing his name in another village. However, there is no benefit in watching the panchayat. The booth where I will stand will continue. Brother Ramzan will not get married. He seems to be flying with me. Let's see what happens. Not after the examination will be seen again. The test is before the vote. No, the education department announced this morning that the election would take place a month later. Oh. Then the examination date was far behind. Yes about four months. All right, you do one thing. Karim is now contesting the election, This time the land has to be sold. Otherwise you don't have to win. It takes money. Now if there is no money, there is no election. All right. And yes listen Niyamat. What. Guys Ginny was telling me to bring meat. Come with me at noon. All right. And keep an eye on the news tab. He is no longer an uncle. Niyamat is going home in the afternoon. At that time some people were going somewhere in groups. Where to go. One calls. Hey Mia brother, come here. Calls and asks, Hey, where are you going? Where is Karim's house again. Why. There is a need. That will happen later. I'll talk to you later. Okay, let's see. Well he can be seen. There are many people in Karim's house today. The backyard is full. People are sitting on the floor. Some people are shouting. It is understandable. A gathering of many people. After a while the tea biscuits came. Bazlu is giving tea to everyone. Nahid is giving biscuits immediately. Fazlu and his members were surprised to see many people. There are so many people without that team. Then what will happen after three months. About sixty percent of the people in the village showed up. It seems that Karim's party has a flat vote. At that time Fazlu stood up in the meeting. Hu hu cleared his throat. Then began to say. "Dear my villagers, welcome and love. We are here today. For the same reason. That is against injustice. To fight against oppression for the development of the region. So we are all villagers to unite and form a team. We have some people to manage the team. Are you by our side? "Everyone said in unison. Yes, we are ready. If necessary, I will give you everything. Fazlu says we don't want any of your goods. We just want one vote. Believe me once. Don't be fooled. We are the committee today or tomorrow." Bakul Master, Khaleq and Nafiz Dr. spoke at the meeting and said that our main weapon is Karim Bhai. I will see Karim Bhai and vote. InshaAllah. The work of the meeting was done. The work of forming the committee tomorrow. There is a lot of trouble. You have to be busy all day. Everyone said in unison. Yes we are ready. If necessary, I will give you all the goods. Fazlu says we don't want any of your goods. Just want a vote. Try it once. Don't cheat. We will form a committee today or tomorrow to campaign. I agree with everyone. Except for a few. Bakul Master, Khaleq and Nafiz Doctor addressed the meeting. And said our main weapon is Karim Bhai. I will vote after seeing Karim Bhai InshaAllah. The speech went on for a long time. About an hour ago. The meeting was held at six o'clock in the evening. The work of forming the committee tomorrow. Lots of trouble. You have to be busy all day. Everyone said in unison. Yes we are ready. If necessary, I will give you all the goods. Fazlu says we don't want any of your goods. Just want a vote. Try it once. Don't cheat. We will form a committee today or tomorrow to campaign. I agree with everyone. Except for a few. Bakul Master, Khaleq and Nafiz Doctor addressed the meeting. And said our main weapon is Karim Bhai. I will vote after seeing Karim Bhai InshaAllah. The speech went on for a long time. About an hour ago. The meeting was held at six o'clock in the evening. The work of forming the committee tomorrow. Lots of trouble. You have to be busy all day. Khaleq and Nafiz spoke. And said our main weapon is Karim Bhai. I will vote after seeing Karim Bhai InshaAllah. The speech went on for a long time. About an hour ago. The meeting was held at six o'clock in the evening. The work of forming the committee tomorrow. Lots of trouble. You have to be busy all day. Khaleq and Nafiz spoke. And said our main weapon is Karim Bhai. I will vote after seeing Karim Bhai InshaAllah. The speech went on for a long time. About an hour ago. The meeting was held at six o'clock in the evening. The work of forming the committee tomorrow. Lots of trouble. You have to be busy all day.

16

It's getting late. Maghrib Azan can be given in a few minutes. At that time Nahid entered Nayan's house. Are you ready? Yes, ready. How long does it take you to come. There was a lot of work at home. What is your job? Let's do a pile of work. Let's go quickly. Mom, I'm going to Rina's house. It will be late to come. People will talk a lot when they go out at night. The people of the village do not understand anything. Their eyes are on the other side of the mind. The people of this village are completely different. All right mom. I go. Let's walk. Yes. Hey, no, there are bicycles. Oh well then. I used to get up and sit down. This is the shed. Began to ride a bicycle. Nayana is sitting in the back. Someone from the village is watching. Nayana says from behind, Well, why did Rina say that she was in trouble? Hey love means a little romance. If there is no romance, what is the benefit of love? I don't want to know why. He came to Rina's house to tell some more stories. The first time I entered the gate of the house was to meet Rina's father. Nahid greeted as soon as he saw it. Assalamu Alaikum Chachaji. Alaikum salam. What's the matter dad this evening. The news is good. Yes uncle. With my soul. As Nayana is the granddaughter of Ramzan Matabbar. Go to the foundation of the house. He went inside the house and entered. There are a few people downstairs. Rina will probably be a guest. Rina's mother saw Nahid and called Rina. Where is Rina? Nahid Nayana has arrived. Nahid is beautifully dressed thinking she will come. Came down. What a happy Rina thinks. Took them from the bottom to the top. And he said to his mother, Mother used to ask Ayesha to make coffee. Oh, that's right. Ayesha Ayesha. Said Ginnima. What to do. Nothing like that. Rina comes home with three coffees. Her friends have arrived. Oh, I'm going. I'm not going right now. All right. Nahid entered Rina's room. He asked the two to sit on the sofa. They sat down. Rina sat down on another sofa. There is a large glass table in front of the sofa. Glass vase on the table. There are a few beautiful flowers. Very nice to see. How are you Rina? Good. You. I'm fine too. However, it seems that he is looking very pale. What's the matter with you Bad body or baby. No body is not bad. That is the pressure of studying in front of the exam. You are covering the fish with greens. Cover him. There is no ban. So if you feel so bad. Ayesha entered the room with coffee. Grandma Coffee. Leave it Something else is needed. No. You go I will call if needed. All right. It will be cold. You take it. Not wanting to eat. Nayana took a sip of a coffee mug. Not wanting to eat, I will feed you. Will give. Why can't I give. You can do that. No, I'm feeding. Listen to this Nao Babu. Now you eat. The two played in the same mug. The last coffee after a few minutes of eating. Tell me your news. What can I say? What do you mean? Did you ever think I'd be better off without you? How can i believe i don't love you anymore I don't mean that. Listen, even if you leave, I will not leave you. I found thousands of seas I was looking for real pearls. And I will throw it away in an instant. There is no price. Rina, I promise you I will never hurt you. I will listen to you all. Rina says I was wrong too. You give me khama. Nayana looked at Rina and said once, Rina I come from below Ray. You guys talk. Rina agrees. Nahid says hey where are you leaving me. Hey, let's meet Grandma. You guys talk. Nayana came out of the house and came downstairs to Ramzan Matabbar's wife. That is to Rina's mother. Rina is very happy. Rina goes to Nahid to come. Sitting next to him. Nahid's chest is getting distant. Rina is excited now. Without wasting time. Puts face to face. Endless kisses. Nahid says nothing more and gives up on Rina. It's all over in a moment. What a beautiful red cheek. However, Nahid could not hold himself this time. He also presented himself in a thrilling way. Kiss eating activities are over. Rina is very happy. Nahid is ashamed. Rina said, I was not comfortable for a few things. But today I feel blessed. Nayana was talking to her grandmother. As the story ends, Grandma says who. Grandma has to go home upstairs. Let's tell Rina. All right. Rina's mother was left to find out why Nayana had come down. I was laughing in my mind. Nayana goes upstairs and enters through the throat. Then I will not go home. Yes, let's go. Rina came home saying goodbye. Rahim and Nader came and told Ramzan Matabbar. Bukul Master did not agree, but joined Karim's team. That's right. It is very difficult. Then I will make Nifaz stand in booth number two. And what will happen in other booths. Those will be seen later. Now I am thinking of these two booths. Let Nifaz know. OK was nominated as a party member. All right. And you will also be parthi. Booths three and four. Another one will be Subid Mia. He will stand at booth number five. That's it. Nader said, Then the work nominated by Parthi is over. Raise as much money as you can. And I will give the rest. How? Those who have been nominated for the party, There will be a separate meeting with them. The party will be in the office. And the People's Party will not give or not. Doesn't feel. He will be seen. The next morning the phone rang in Nahid's pocket. In the pocket of jeans pants. Big smartphone. Hello. Tell me. What's the matter Phone so early in the morning. Nothing like that. Oh that's good. What are you doing This dad is out of the discussion for the election so I'm going. Oh. That's good. Your father is fighting against his father-in-law. You will get married. That is God's affair. But I always want to get Rina. This Janis seems to have been stirring up another exciting greed of mine since that day's incident. True. I'm not really lying to you. Well, Nayana, you used to say that this is what love is all about. I don't know him. These eyes will talk to you later. I understand. Lots of work now. Ok i will talk later All right. At that time Karim called. Where is Nahid Baba? Come on Yes, Dad. Bakul Master said, Now you have to enter Yasin's house in front. Yes master. Fazlu said, is there Fazlu brother or not. After a while the answer came. Yes i am Come home. Entered with all the team inside. And Nafiz the doctor said, You see, brother, you know everything. Nothing to say. Karim Bhai is the guest of our booth. The vote must be given. Yes, brother, of course. No worries. Brother, you have to vote for any brand. The Election Commission has not given any mark yet. Nomination file tomorrow. Run election programs in the neighborhoods. Almost all the neighborhoods received a huge vote response. Opposition groups called for a boycott of the by-elections. But they were not satisfied with the faces of the common people. About seventy percent of people are dissatisfied. Karim's party has given party in every booth. Parthi has given in five parliaments. Or selected. The documents will be submitted tomorrow by Karim's party, the Socialist Party of Thamathampur (SPF). Ramzan Matabbar broke his old party president's misunderstanding and returned to the People's Party. Their party has already taken place. The People's Party of Ramadan has submitted its nomination today. Local video k. Sadeq Matabbar himself stood. In the last parliament. They have also been given partisans but nominations have been submitted Tomorrow. The day of submission of the Socialist Party.

16

The day was Tuesday. Karim's party is working in the morning. Abdul Karim Sheikh, the party president, i.e. the candidate for the second parliament. Co-president means one

Dr. Nafiz Ali, a Member of Parliament. Editor Fazlu Sheikh. Doing all the papers. Meanwhile, Sadeq has already arranged the work. Because he knows everything. Since a few days ago he was the Member of Parliament for the Eleventh Parliament. Now that the Panchayat is new, he is a Member of Parliament for the Second Parliament. Moreover, he has been in politics for a long time. Mature man from there. Needless to say. The government has changed the date of the examination. The government is playing with the future of the students in its own interest. Nahid's bad test would have been better if it had happened earlier. Dad could have worked on the election. Dad must win. Then many things will come in handy. Nahid and Sujan's former friend Sujan has now joined hands with Sadeq. Now he has got the post of youth president of the party. It is difficult to see his mood. He is also going viral saying that he is willing to sacrifice himself for the party. Some youths are also planning to commit hooliganism together. He continued to use obscene language in his speech. People think Hatred is spreading. He has become a bully by becoming the leader of the youth committee. Who stops him. Nayana and Rina are coming to Nayana's house. Hey you What matters is where it goes. It's not right to talk to you. Why. What have I done wrong? No fault. Have you ever looked for me? Itching the head and saying yay means. Not having to work for Dad's election. I have to do meetings, processions etc. So. Oh. So will you forget about me? Choosing against father-in-law. Don't feel ashamed. What a shame again. Father-in-law's booth is different. We have no political relationship with father-in-law. Or love your dad enough. Respect. Of course he is. I told you something about that. Of course not. Let's go for a walk tomorrow. Where. Let's go. Hey, don't tell me where to go. A: A: A: In the dream park. What to do with there. He will be seen. You can. Eyes will go. Is that so? Yes. Okay today. I'll let you know in the evening. I went to the Bhola shop with sweet money. Sear will tell. Let me know. Let's go now.

16

Today is the day to submit the nomination file or nomination paper of the Socialist Party. There was paperwork and some party work. They are finished. Now it is time to go to the BDO office and submit. So in the office of the election officer present with the party workers and supporters. Many are submitting. And after a few he will read the line. Time goes by. Has been in line for a long time. Being one. Then it will be his. The submission of the previous party is over. The line fell. The papers were handed over to the election official. The official is verifying. Looking carefully at the paper. The officer asked, Mister, what is your name? My name is Karim Sheikh. Here I see your new team. Yes. All right. Your booth number two. Parthi is number two. The brand is the fan. Take this slip of registration card. Go to room number eleven and sign and take the stamp. From the Chief Officer. Thank you sir. Karim and his entourage had to enter the chief officer's room. Prohibition issued. Only party and party leaders will come. Since Karim is the party leader and Parthi himself. So he went alone. The official signed to show the registration. And gave Karim a paper. There are ticks in many places. Karim, the fan marker Parthi, signed there. This is the first time he is a party member. Nomination papers were submitted with great fanfare. And Karim gave a special speech to the party to ensure the smooth running of the electoral process. Karim gave an open speech today. The right to speak in this way belongs to the Matabbars in the village Was. New face today. But not once did he criticize the opposition. He has repeatedly made people understand their own responsibilities and development. The illiterate people of the village have never heard such a good speech. Along with communal and party violence and provocative statements, the people have turned their attention to the vote. Believing in new faces this time. Opposition groups called for a boycott of the assembly. Provoking people. Karim's opposition parties are frustrated. Few people in the meeting. Ramzan Matabbar is also scared. Why not. The people of the village are not listening to him now. The people of the village understand how much they have cheated. People have turned their attention to voting by making provocative statements. Believing in new faces this time. Opposition groups called for a boycott of the assembly. Provoking people. Karim's opposition parties are frustrated. Few people in the meeting. Ramzan Matabbar is also scared. Why not. The people of the village are not listening to him now. The people of the village understand how much they have cheated. People have turned their attention to voting by making provocative statements. Believing in new faces this time. Opposition groups called for a boycott of the assembly. Provoking people. Karim's opposition parties are frustrated. Few people in the meeting. Ramzan Matabbar is also scared. Why not. The people of the village are not listening to him now. The people of the village understand how much they have cheated.

19

Anyway a lot of trouble now. Voting time. However, the work of Sadeq and Ramzan's team is over. I think the prominent people of the village. But it is better to throw away the old teams and show the new ones. The election campaign is in full swing. Sadeq, Karim and Ramadan. The propaganda of all three parties is deadly. Nahid and Rina's complex love is going on with him. Now everything is fine. Although Nahid's father fought against Ramadan, Ramzan Matabbar loves Nahid enough. Nahid had two acres of land inside Sadeq's area. Sadeq can't swallow it. Because both are now people of two poles. Who sees whom. And there are a few days of elections. Meanwhile, Ramzan Matabbar entered Nahid's house. Where are you? Chhota Karim of Ramadan Matabbar. About seven years will be short. Again the influential person is from the village. Karim came out of the house. Seeing this, Ramzan Matabbar is standing in the backyard. Cane in hand. With luxury. Luxury is the servant of Ramadan. His grant is not less but. The village has saved a lot. Of course with the help of Ramadan. But no one knows that except Ramadan and luxury. Ramzan Matabbarai forbade Bilas K. Nahid's father Karim said, The dust of my elder brother's feet is in my house. What good fortune I have. Koi re nahid chair de karta moshai ke. Nahid salutes Rina's father. And quickly brought a chair. Nahid goes home. To mother Tell mother that Ramadan uncle has come. I told my mother to make coffee. Nahid's mother went to make coffee. In the kitchen. I understand, Ray Karim, You have a good time now so I left. To visit your house. Grab this sweet pot. Bauma to keep the ball. So he handed over the luxury to Karim. Karim eats Vyabachaka. Big brother why sweet pot in my house. Why are you scared? What I can't bring. You can do that but you are our master. We eat your land by sharing contract. Don't shame us. These were the things that came to my mind when I was contesting the elections and fighting against everyone. Who am I going to fight against? Listen, skip that. I think everyone is a bad person. But this guy has done no work right without me. If you do politics, everyone will be bad. This is real. The first name in politics will be felt later. However, he is your personal matter. There is no problem in my booth. Vote for me. Master, I know him. Okay, you don't have to do it anymore. This time I have to say goodbye. How master. Hey, I have brought about Rina's marriage with Nahid. No Rina Master. Master again. Why isn't the elder brother or brother leaving? No, it's not. Listen to my daughter's marriage proposal. What are you saying It's not possible, big brother. Listen, everything is possible. I don't say socialist, and I don't say it on my face. In fact, it is not big brother. You are the owner people. We do not go with you. I know that too. I don't have to explain. Listening to these words is a luxury. Luxury is the source of eating vimri. Yes. Ramzan Matabbar says, why is that hapless ha. Shut up At that time Nahid came with coffee. Gone with the coffee. He was listening to everything from the house. And he knows everything. What else to say. Whether anyone has status in this village or not. Coffee tea but everyone has it at home. Because coffee is cultivated here. Do you understand? No i mean I didn't know they both loved each other. Listen, I may be bad, but that's a personal matter. But it is up to them who will marry my son and daughter. I love my son and daughter properly. For their happiness, I am willing to have relations with the enemy. All right, let's get up. I will come another day. Let's get elected. After the election, either marriage will be discussed. Eighteen years have passed since this time. Nahid is also close to Ekushey. I will take care of them through marriage. You don't care. No fear. I'm not as bad as you think. Let's go. Saying this, Ramzan left the coffee mug and left the house. Karim calls Nahid and Nahid's mother. Come here, Nahid's mother. Nahid also came. Know or say. Mr. Moral said, Is that right? Yes, Dad. I love Rina. Did you have a bad head? For the love of the rich man's daughter. Nahid doesn't talk anymore. The head is bowed. After a few reprimands, he went inside the house. The whole thing is told to Nahid's mother i.e. Karim's wife. After hearing everything, Nahid's mother Surmila says, then Mr. Matabbar should be told well. So much good news. Yes, that's right. Do you agree, Nahid's father? Why not agree, when Mr. Matabbar himself comes and offers. Nahid's mother says that the girl is also very beautiful. Yes it sounds very intelligent. Educated. Okay I'm going out a little bit. While Matabbar is walking down the road, Bilas is saying, well, sir, I will say something. Tell me. Guys, sir, are you crazy? What do you mean? Where is the proposal to marry the fakir's son with the mother. Again by itself. Boo: Boo: I can't believe it. He doesn't have to obey you. We are still alive. They are not happy. And what if he is the son of a fakir? The boy is good. Besides, I have no shortage of money. Something will happen to me or not. You don't have to worry about that. You do your job. Yet the master. Luxury goes silent.

Chapter 3

20

Various political riots are going on. The BDO office was bombed. The police force could not bring control there. Later, the police of the local police station called the police high command office. However, the phone calls towards the end of the day. At that time some people were killed and injured. However, the ruling party did this evil deed on the orders of the local government. Opposition camps could not field candidates anywhere else in the panchayat elections. In the Thamathampur panchayat election, the party had submitted nomination papers in advance. Ruling party thugs also raided the homes of opposition members of the ruling party. The police also go to bully. However eventually the police came from the head office, a lot of police. Arrived in the net. Shields, Kadani gas sticks, etc. have been brought. Water car, so that it can be stopped with water. Police came to the camp of the anti-stick manusagulikei of Murray, The water kills. Many were killed and their heads were blown off. Even former professor and MLA Nasiruddin Sahib was killed and his head was torn off by the ruling party's police force. The word of hooliganism fell in the name of the party in the district. There is no party in any booth. Those who submit nomination papers, Ruling party thugs and police forces forced them to withdraw their nomination papers. Where will the common people stand. Where to go. Wailing in the country. No food. No industry. No education system. Leaders are looting political benefits. When uneducated people become leaders, the country goes wild. This is what is happening in Lucia country. Lucia's prime minister caused terror in the country's panchayat elections. Anarchy and horror descended on the original Lucia. However, the Thamathampur panchayat did not have such an impact. Because the panchayat has just been divided. Before the first election of partition, the government fed the masses. But it has dismissed the ruling party chief. Or they didn't. But the people of Thamathampur will vote for Karim's party, the Socialist Party. The people of the village have been united. There were no riots. The ruling party is the party of Ramadan Matabbar. He has been ruling the village for a long time. This time it has shrunk a lot. However, the opposition camp, that is, the girl's marriage to Karim's son Ramzan Matabbar is thinking. The election will come in a few days. No more time. Meanwhile, Sadeq is scattering money like a squirrel. He must win. Because if you can't win the panchayat election, it is a matter of shame. Besides, the road to big income will die on the field. Time is short again. Sadeq's sons are engaged in public service. Weaving sari is brought to give to the girls of the house. Quintal quintal bought rice, pulses, oil etc. To give to people. So that ordinary people vote for Sadeq. Sadeq's children are jumping as soon as he arrives. They also tricked Sadeq and removed sari, rice, pulses, oil etc. Fifty percent distributed in the village. Fifty percent removed for themselves. He did not even let Sadeq know. Of course, the boy has done all the hops. Scattering money is like a murky murky. He must win. Because if you can't win the panchayat election, it is a matter of shame. Besides, the road to big income will die on the field. Time is short again. Sadeq's sons are engaged in public service. Weaving sari is brought to give to the girls of the house. Quintal quintal bought rice, pulses, oil etc. To give to people. So that ordinary people vote for Sadeq. Sadeq's children are jumping as soon as he arrives. They also tricked Sadeq and removed sari, rice, pulses, oil etc. Fifty percent distributed in the village. Fifty percent removed for themselves. He did not even let Sadeq know. Of course, the boy has done all the hops. Scattering money is like a murky murky. He must win. Because if you can't win the panchayat election, it is a matter of shame. Besides, the road to big income will die on the field. Time is short again. Sadeq's sons are engaged in public service. Weaving sari is brought to give to the girls of the house. Quintal quintal bought rice, pulses, oil etc. To give to people. So that ordinary people vote for Sadeq. Sadeq's children are jumping as soon as he arrives. They also tricked Sadeq and removed sari, rice, pulses, oil etc. Fifty percent distributed in the village. Fifty percent removed for themselves. He did not even let Sadeq know. Of course, the boy has done all the hops. Sadeq's sons are gone. Weaving sari is brought to give to the girls of the house. Quintal quintal bought rice, pulses, oil etc. To give to people. So that ordinary people vote for Sadeq. Sadeq's children are jumping as soon as he arrives. They also tricked Sadeq and removed sari, rice, pulses, oil etc. Fifty percent distributed in the village. Fifty percent removed for themselves. He did not even let Sadeq know. Of course, the boy has done all the hops. Sadeq's sons are gone. Weaving sari is brought to give to the girls of the house. Quintal quintal bought rice, pulses, oil etc. To give to people. So that ordinary people vote for Sadeq. Sadeq's children are jumping as soon as he arrives. They also tricked Sadeq and removed sari, rice, pulses, oil etc. Fifty percent distributed in the village. Fifty percent removed for themselves. He did not even let Sadeq know. Of course, the boy has done all the hops. Ghunaksare did not even know. Of course, the boy has done all the hops. Ghunaksare did not even know. Of course, the boy has done all the hops.

21

That day was Monday. The school holidays ended a week ago. The school is now locked. Speaking of high school. The Election Commission is sending troops. And first of all this school i.e. Rina will come to Nadid's school. Because there is only one high school in the panchayat. The army is sending BDOs everywhere. Stitched cut pants shirt. Tall tall man. He has a big rifle around his neck. There will be about one and a half thousand in front of the gate of Namal High School. There is no doubt about that. There is a big gentleman. What did he say by pointing at them? What is the elder brother of the police station saying in English with Mr. Abdus Salam. Not well understood. Yet Batbabu says no. The school caretaker came and opened the school door. The school has already been cleaned. Of course, it was done during Ramadan. He was still the head of the region a few days ago. When the new panchayat was divided, he became the hartakar. As a result, he is the big man there. Finally Ramzan Matabbar arrived. Inspector He said to Babu, everything is fine. Barababu greeted him and said. What if the police. Mr. Salam falls at the feet of the leaders. Because he has to work. Since now the new region president. There was no presidency before. Before the election, there was a disagreement with the old panchayat president. Ramzan Matabbar said, we have legally divided the panchayat. Therefore, the president will be different. But the president wanted his son to be the president of Thamathampur panchayat. So Ramzan Matabbar was bent over. So Ramzan was forced to become the new party panchayat president from the block office. The policy of the party is that no one is above the party. Ramadan does not know English. Didn't even study. What else is read in a newspaper. Ramzan Matabbar studied up to second class in primary school. The old man said let's talk. The leader speaks. Let's go. Yes go. You go with me, I do not understand the language. Barababu and Ramzan went and talked for a while. They are changing some clothes. Some are having coffee. Ramzan Matabbar, Barababu and the army chief are laughing. Eating coffee too. There are many words between them. Barababu is translating between Ramadan and the army chief. It's a good story. There is no Parthi in other places. There are some places where the opposition camp is very tough. The ruling party deprived the people of Lucia of their basic right to vote. This created anarchy in the current government of the country. Great wrongdoing. Which is the work of a dictator. But it is not right in a democratic country. The government needed to understand. Many are saying that this is what happens when a woman is the head of state, while others are saying that who knows, maybe one day she will be expelled from the country. Various criticisms are coming from the mouths of common people. With whom did Aslam form the government? The press is all in his possession. Again, some are saying that who knows, maybe one day he will be expelled from the country. Various criticisms are coming from the mouths of common people. With whom did Aslam form the government? The press is all in his possession.

22

The great relationship between Nahid and Rina is impossible to break. Fully iron furniture. Which is not breaking. It can be bent only with iron. Some members of Ramzan's party are saying that Matabbar is building a relationship with Karim. With her daughter. Ramadan's head is completely gone. What is the point of meeting with the enemy. Of course, the whispers are in the inner court of the party. Ramadan Matabbar doesn't care. Rina is getting up early in the morning. Mother asked where to go. Where is your future son-in-law's house again? There is a need. But you're overdoing it, Rina. Where is mother? I am a beautiful friend of Nahid. I can go. Where is the difficulty. Yes i will go After marriage. Your father told you to get married. We have no problem with that. At that time Matabbar entered the room. What's so significant about a goat's head? " What's the matter Where to go. Yes, Dad. Or to go somewhere. No. Future father-in-law's house. What is he? Father-in-law without growing up. What a matter. I can't say all that. Parents are not letting go. Dad it's not unfair. Yes it is wrong, of course it is wrong. Dad then go. Go mom. Saying this, he turned his hand on the girl's head. Rina left. Rina's mother said, "Well, since when have you been so good?" Walking around his wife's neck, he said, "Look, Ginny is very old, I did not feel good to anyone. Or I started to get better from today. I think I will withdraw the nomination. Ordinary people or good people get development. I am leaving politics tomorrow. I've made up my mind. No one calls me good. Ginny said, "I know you haven't done anything wrong." I know you have developed. I know all about you. Listen, I have decided to leave the village before the election. I will go home to the city. And what will be the future of Rina. What will happen next Rina is the girl of this village. I will get married here. And your father's words. I can't, Ginny. I couldn't. We will make some arrangements before leaving. I don't think so. I will get married after the election. I will resign from politics tomorrow. Then it will be. All the gold and grains planted in Abbajan must be around two hundred crores. They are in that house. The key to the ark was given to me before Abbajan died. Yes i know At that time I was the new wife of Oibari. Abbajan made you home in the village for your little mistake. He also gave two hundred bighas of land. Yes, that's a long time ago, about thirty years ago. Well, now go to the house will not be upset. For the village. Of course it will. But I will go to my birthplace. I will die there. Even then we can get peace. Abbajan could not accept because we had a relationship while studying in college. So introduce yourself to the society as a fool. Exclude those things. I need to write a letter. Must be sent to the Election Commission Department. You will easily forget. Soil tension. How many villages are you? Fell in love You have done so much in the village, but the people of the village are cunning. And what will happen to that work. What will happen next. People will get it the way they get it. No problem.

23

Hey mom you're in our house. Why can't I come? Why not. Of course I can, mother. You are such a good girl. My daughter did not give me one like you. Nahid does not listen to me. Big boy. Why aunty, everyone says so. But he doesn't listen to his mother. Read and read. Listen to your father. Oh so. Well Aunt Nahid is not at home. There is no bridge. When out of the house. Went to put the festoon. Aunt then Nahid is joining politics. Tell me what else to say mother. The father is not doing politics, but the boy is getting involved in politics. Why doesn't the uncle forbid. Examination in front of him. But not like before. Now voting. Many are saying that if they win the vote, they will pass. Yes, aunty will say that. The board is Nahid's uncle. I know everyone was talking. What do they know? What the people of the village understand. At that time Nahid came. Then he said to his mother, Mother, give me rice. Got very hungry. Rina saw them coming home. Still did not say anything. Sat down to eat. Rina is waiting at Nahid's house. Walking. There are photos on the wall. Lots of books on the reading table. He sat down in the chair. I looked at the math book several times. Closed again. Walking. Leaving his hands behind his back, he is holding his fingers. He went again and sat on Nahid's bed. Chit lay down. Rolling upside down again, he is thinking with his hands on the pillow and his chin on the pillow. When will you come home? Thinking for a while. Thinking, Nahid came and shouted. Uh-huh. Nahid was looking out the window. He came a long time ago. Seeing Nahid rolling, it was all over. The mind is now playing in the tidal waters. Without saying a word, he slammed the door and jumped on Rina's chest. Nahid is lying on some soft sponge. Rina says what matters is that the truthful mind wants something today. Oh no no. I can't get anything. No. Yours Like does not agree with the truthful. Why. You are not truthful. Rina is still lying on her body like soft fluffy butter. The bodies of the two are burning hot. Maybe in a while the Kalavaishakhi storm may rise. Talking hot. Rina is lying on her chest talking. Just keeping the head on the breast. What are you saying That's right, you don't touch me. What happened today was that I had to jump on my chest. Look, I don't know all that. Today it seems that some kind of hot air is flowing in my body. It's a book. The body heat of women is determined by the provider. Whoever comes here once will have a bad head. Nahid started kissing without saying anything else. Lips, cheeks, throat, abdomen, chest, etc. Then Rina is just making some noise. Rina grabbed Nahid's back with full force. There is a different kind of peace. Very exciting thing. Rina said to herself, Let Baba Babushona understand the irritation of the mind even if it is late. Nahid is still going to kiss. It seems that the mad dog is getting meat and eating it. Rina spread her arms and legs on the bed. Nahid who has destroyed himself. Nahid is playing the game as he pleases. The love affair lasted for a long time. Rina is curling up. But Konkani is not angry. Happy groaning. Nahid went inside the house. What I thought came inside the house again. Rina forgive me. What have I done? I'm extremely sorry. Hey sorry why. I don't mean that I made a big mistake and Rina sat down at my feet. Hey hey what are you doing I need to reward you for your bravery. I was very happy and hugged Nahid. He kissed her neck. Rina looks happy. This moment looks much more beautiful than before. Very beautiful. What else do you want in life? Talk for a while. The story is. Nahid is coming to push Rina forward. At that time Karim came and stood up At the front gate of the house. Seeing Rina, he said, hey, when is the mother? Stay home. No, uncle, whatever you read at home. Uncle will come to our house but. Hey, I'm coming from your house. True. But a tragedy. There is news, mother. No matter how bad the village. The decision to leave the village was not good for you. Leaving home means what uncle is saying. I don't understand anything. When I was coming to the meeting, your father called me. Hey, Mister, where are you coming from? There are some urgent matters with you. What are you talking about, Lord? There are some important things to come. I went to your house. Your mother immediately treated me properly. Then you said, "Mr. Behay, we are leaving you a resource." Leaving means. Where are you going? Doesn't mean we're going to town tomorrow. Why don't you want to stay here. Everyone is doing bad things in my name. They are not looking with good eyes. There are many reasons. So guys don't want to give the girl in your house. Suddenly Ramzan Matabbar grabbed Karim's hand. Brother, you agree with me. And we will come from there for a few days to test. What are you saying. It is difficult to agree to marry No. But sir you will not leave the village. No, I have to go. I understood your father a lot but he said the same thing. But you will marry Nahid. I agreed. You will get married after the vote. Rina heard the words and ran towards the house.

24

Daddy Daddy. You are at home. What are you talking about, mother? Why are you calling me Abba Abba? Why is it so late to go to Nahid's house. That's where Dad went. He has gone to Haripara. Why. I don't know. Why there in the evening. I don't know. Tell him something. I will say yes. Or are we going to town tomorrow? Yes. Who will tell Karim uncle. Oh. Yes, I'm going. But you have no problem marrying Nahid. I know why I'm going. I don't know. Rina sighed and shook the stairs of the house. What a surprise. Saying this, he went to his house.

25

The next morning a VIP car was coming. With paved roads of the village. Many people are yawning. Many are saying, Where will the car go? Such a beautiful expensive car. He used to say who is going home. One said who knows where he is going. The car went a little and came back again. Those who were sitting in the corner of the three heads called them the driver of the car. And where does Mr. Ramzan make his uncle's house. No Ramadan. That party does not split. And the house of Ramzan Matabbar. Maybe. Go a little further to the left. When you go, you will see a mud two-storey house in front. Thank you Mister. The car was moving. The car stopped right at home. Ramzan picked up the nomination papers at the BDO office in Haripara yesterday evening. From there there is no problem now. Ramzan Matabbar is leaving the village five days before the election. The driver went and entered the house. Kakababu Kakababu or not. Hey, you eyes. Yes, Dad sent me. How are you aunt? There was gossip. What else to take. A few things. A small iron box given by Ramzan's father. An old stick. Some clothing. Rina has all her dress books Took things to use. About two suitcases. The driver left his luggage in the back of the car. Ramzan told Bilas with the house key. I left the luxury house in your care and took care of it. You cultivate ten bighas of land. And this is the home address. Let's go for a walk. How? Bilas repeatedly stares at Ramzan's face. Bilas burst into tears. Babu followed us. Ramzan Matabbar also cried. Rahid called at night even after Nahid heard it in his father's mouth yesterday. Said we are leaving the village tomorrow, see you if you can. Rina Nahid's grief There is no end to it. The lover knows what happens when the person he loves leaves. Nahid came. Uncle is leaving. Yes, Dad. But you also go for a walk. Bilas has an address. Moreover, Rina will know everything by calling on her mobile. How? Rina and Nahid are staring blankly. Ramzan's wife has already got in the car. Matabbar first lifted Rina to the middle seat. However, all three are sitting in the middle seat. Everyone said goodbye to Nahid and the house staff and left for the city.

26

Everyone in the village was shocked. What's the matter Matabbar left without informing anyone. He did not even inform his neighbor Sadeq. Although Sadeq was in the opposition camp, they were friends. Still did not inform. Only Nahid and Nahid's father know the village. And the employees of Matabbar. Many are saying let the disaster go. Many are also expressing regret. He did nothing in the village. Has done. Has made a lot of progress. Seto never lost the vote. People can't think. Meanwhile, the report came to the party's vice president. Ramadan has picked up the nomination papers. Parthi cannot be given now. The block president of the People's Party is in trouble. What else to do. And there is not much time for voting. Everyone is waiting for the election ready. The military has arrived. In every booth.

26

Nahid is upset. He has never had such a condition in his life. Feeling we have 'Run out of gas' emotionally. Time has driven Rina away from him. On the other hand, wondering if Ramzan uncle went to the city to not marry Rina with me. So did everyone in their house play with me? Boo: Boo: What are you thinking? That can't be. Rina is mine. Nayana is tying her legs. He came closer and said. What Ray is here alone in the afternoon. What are you doing What else can I do, friend, you know my life is hard. Time took Rina away from me. Hey, are you thinking the opposite? No reason to worry. Really yes yes yes. Let's go home. There are no parents to tell the story. Mamabari has gone. Let's have at least a cup of coffee. What do you say? Yeah Al that sounds pretty crap to me, Looks like BT aint for me either. No sinner is needed. Why can't I pay. Yes, of course. Why can't a friend kiss another friend. Exactly. Let's go. Chats can be given with movies. Oh, what a wonderful way to screw people over. How beautiful it would have been. Hey, you have your belongings. After marriage, there is no problem in chetepute khas. Let's go now. Nahid and Nayana walked along the narrow road of the village with their hands on their necks to Nayana's house. If Rina had been there at that time. How beautiful it would have been. Hey, you have your belongings. After marriage, there is no problem in chetepute khas. Let's go now. Nahid and Nayana walked along the narrow road of the village with their hands on their necks to Nayana's house. If Rina had been there at that time. How beautiful it would have been. Hey, you have your belongings. After marriage, there is no problem in chetepute khas. Let's go now. Nahid and Nayana walked along the narrow road of the village with their hands on their necks to Nayana's house.

26

Rina's car stopped at Baharpur. It's a big city. Many rich people live here. It is not suitable for the poor to live here. HiFi people live here. There is a big university here. The name of the university is Rabindra Nazrul University. The shortcut name is RN University. A four-storey house next to the university. White house. Nice to see. Homes worth crores of rupees. You can see. Rina's father asked. Who could this house be? Baba Ramzan Matabbar died for a while. Rina asked again. The original owner of the house was Awal Hossain Chowdhury. Who is he Mother has a lot of time to know all this. Keep quiet Slowly the car went and stopped near the white house. Huge house. At least it will be a house worth fifty crore rupees. Everyone went down. Many are standing at the gate with garlands. Some people say that Babu has come. Babu is gone. Lots of people. Before entering the house, he greeted Ramzan Matabbar with a garland of flowers. Rina So surprised. Thinking in my mind. What's the matter Then father, is there anyone in this house? No, it can't be. Dad doesn't know how to read much. Matabbar people of the village. And this house can never be owned. There is an old man sitting inside the house. Ramzan went to him and cried as a child. The old woman is also crying. The two of them strangled each other. Your father is so angry. Where did you leave us? I have been around for thirty years. When will he come? Finally angry Kamal Baba. Auntie, you haven't even thought about your old father, mother. Don't say anything. Cries. Go mother go home. How would you be if you had a father-in-law today, mother? The old man took Rina to his house. On the third floor. What a beautiful house. Many decorated houses. Which is difficult to appreciate. The old man told Rina, It must be Granddaughter Solomon. Yes uncle. This is your granddaughter. And you have grandchildren abroad. Where America. There will be a doctor. Oh well. Booma, this is not the key. I can't keep it anymore. The big trouble is. Why uncle you are our elder. I will follow your advice. Keep the key with you. I have another day. And Sulaiman, rest for a day or two. Later the company will understand everything from Akash. Little uncle i.e. younger brother of Awal Hossain Chowdhury. Free: Children. There is a adopted daughter. Akash is married. He lives in this house. Akkash is the son-in-law of this house and Chowdhury is the director general of group industry. The real owner of this house is Sulaiman Chowdhury alias Ramzan Matabbar. He holds a Masters in Commerce from Oxford University in the United States. He left the house at the word of his father. He bequeathed all his father's property to Solomon, and to his younger brother. Awala Chowdhury was the last word of this house. Then little uncle. And now Ramadan. Rina found out in a few days. That they are not actually village people. And my father is not uneducated. Dad is a big educated man. Dad left home for Grandpa. Now our whole house. No one shares here. My father even owns a big company. Home. No one shares here. My father even owns a big company. Home. No one shares here. My father even owns a big company.

29

Election day has come. People are ready to vote in the morning. Gave the agent of his own team. Help center opened. Nanan is making noise. Leaders are rushing. Voting is going on peacefully. Big leaders are also coming to the booth. Going to see. The ruling party has no party in booth number two. In the afternoon. Fifty percent of the vote has just fallen. From time to time Bakul Master, Sadeq, Nafiz Master, Atiq Saheb, Karim and many more. The leaders of their respective parties are moving. Nahid is also turning again and again. He has been given a lot of work. And there is no search for Ramadan Matabbar. People are coming to vote. Someone is going again. It was getting late in the afternoon. Voting ends at booths two and four. Ballot papers are packing. Booth number one is almost done. The vote was peaceful. This is the first time a panchayat has been divided and a peaceful vote has taken place. This time there was no disturbance due to extra military. The Central Army was something. The general public has been talking about elections for a long time, But the election is over. Leaders who have work now. It's all over. Results after three months. A lot of the time. Who will win and who will lose. See you then.

Chapter 4

30

Time is running out. Rina has not called yet. The previous number does not call. The switch says stop. Heavy hard. Rina doesn't call either. Ten days have passed since the election. Exam within a few days. I don't even mind teaching. I go out to read again. That scorpion rolled. Kissed, he repeatedly leaned towards the bed. Every time he has a chest pain. Forced to go to another room with the book. He doesn't even come to bed at night. Feels bad. No contact. Rina goes to the village house. Bilas asks, well uncle uncle went with the address that can be given. And address. Yes, the address is one but nothing is written in it. Only "Baharpur" is written. . Nothing else. Oh, there in the city. Thirty miles. Where to look for such a big city. This is the luxury. How do you think he will marry you. It's a matter of the rich. You can't have a relationship with them. He left because he didn't want to go with you. Exclude that. Will study Will cultivate. Be happy by getting married.

Nahid heard these words and went to Amban with tears in her eyes to spend some time alone. Sitting alone is questioning himself. What's wrong with you? They are deceitful. Poor people like us do not agree with them. Yet the mind does not mean. Talk about love. Chest burst into tears. Tears flowed. At such a time a rat is coming out of the hole with something in its mouth. It's a lot of fun. The rat was white. Some skin color has been lost due to soil in the hole. He threw the shiny object on the ground. The sun is shining through the gaps in the leaves of the mango tree on the shiny object. The thing is getting brighter in it. Nahid was some distance away. Seeing the matter from there. The rat went back to the hole and another one came. Went a few times and brought a few. Nahid was startled as he approached. Arabs are so many gold coins. Where did it come from? He rubbed the coins in his hand. So much gold. What a pleasure. Happy Don't hold on anymore. He took it in his pocket. And sat down to grab the rat. The trap was thin. After waiting for a long time, the rat was finally caught. A beautiful mouse. Looks like a polite rat. Making new home. Brought home. Nahid did not tell anyone about the coin. I haven't remembered love all day. It's just gold. I'm thinking of staying there a lot. Will go at night. Go alone. No one is needed. Not even Dad. Then around noon. He picked up a large shovel, a spade, a torch, and a large sword. Under the bed at home. It's getting late. It's getting late. Nahid thinks that the restlessness is increasing so much. Nahid never got courage in his chest. But today it looks like a huge hero. There is no such thing as fear. It was about seven o'clock at night. Ignoring my parents, I went out of the house. Why not. Sunsan. Very empty. Then who will be in the garden tonight. Who will see. No one will know. Sujan's mango orchard. Bismillah Allahu Akbar shouted. Nothing to dig No. Where is the gold? But don't dig into the rat hole. After a while the head went into play, which the rat bar did. Then you have to dig towards his hole. Yes, that's what he did. Digging came right up to the store. It will take a lot of space. He traveled home three times.

31

The next day no one was allowed to enter Nahid's house. And forbade anyone else to enter here. Locked the house and went to the market. Karim's wife, that is, Nahid's mother. What happened to the boy? He doesn't do that. Didn't even give a broom in the morning. Locked up again and went somewhere. Nahid brought a rod cutting machine from the market. The window of the house closes the door. Began to cut the floor. Worked for about an hour and five minutes. Cement was brought home. Earlier there was cement work in the house. Not made for election. Finished working. The house is empty. Two days later it is normal again. Who let the parents go home. But don't give it to anyone else. My Rina came to this room to say something. She's gone from me. His memories are involved. So I don't want anyone to enter my house. Parents know how much they love Rina. So he does not allow anyone to enter his house. Not so much with friends. Only with eyes. Wandering, Talking with eyes. Mete stays. The study has given more attention than before. No worries now. There is a lot of tension in love. But where to find him. Where to look in the big city. Maybe he's looking for me too. But parents are not afraid. But I am not the one to give up. And now I have everything.

32

Exam tomorrow. The girls' center has fallen elsewhere. BB Pal School. Nahid's center is Nazrullab Vidyapeeth. As a result, it is difficult to meet. Even if it was close again. It will take about three hours. In that case it is impossible to meet again. Love is no longer understood. He kept the sadness in his mind. What else to do. There is nothing to do. As a result, the tests went well. Results after three months. Voting and test results will be together. Maybe a few days ago. But it's great fun.

33

There is no work now. It would be better to travel. Nahid gives time with eyes. But the two are just friends. But nothing else. Very good friend Their friendship is incomparable. Hanging out with more friends.

One day parents and Nahid are talking in the afternoon. At that time Nahid said. Well, how much does it cost to buy a house in Dad's town? It is about two to four crores. Oh. I understand why Ray is a hobby of buying a house in the city. No, Dad. Well Dad we can't buy. Far crazy boy we are poor people. Where can I get so much money? Get rid of those dreams. Think real. Saying this, Baba stopped Nahid. Nahid takes the rat to Sujan's garden.

34

Rina is thinking a lot about when the test results will come out. When will you get married? I will never be able to meet Nahid. Nahid will die without finding me. Oh God, I will not get lost in following my father's advice. Rina's father told Rina, Listen, mother, get out as long as the result is not out. Have fun with new friends here. Eat whatever you like. Give Nahid a pistachio now. Let the batter burn for a while. I will bring it here after the result. Will study here. I will give you a good post job. Will serve as Managing Director. Then when I get older, I will take immediate relief with marriage. I have to increase my chest pain to make my father happy. Who knows how my favorite is. Can't even call. The father put his hand on his head and took an oath. I will give the boy a surprise. He is very good but my mind is no longer in the situation. What can be done. I got into big trouble. There is no way out.

35

When Nahid came to the garden, he hugged the rat and smiled a few times. Playing alone with the baby rat. The rat also obeyed Nahid. Nahid doesn't go anywhere without K. Don't run away. Playing with him all the time. Nice thing. I have heard that Badar, elephant, khorgos etc. mean pets. So to say absolutely forest rats. I have heard again that there is a kind of rat in human pet. But it is absolutely unbelievable that the forest rats will be domesticated.

Nahid now wants to buy a house in Sonarpur. Why or why not. Now he is the ocean of money. Even a million times more millionaires than Ramzan Matabbar. Alone in many ways. I'll do it, I'll do it. Then I will teach Rina too. He could have called me once and told me that I didn't like him anymore. Could send a letter. Bilas Kakar's words are true. He is right. Rinara has left home not to get married. But Rina also has a lot of faults. Could have let me know once. The test is over today. It's been about fifteen days. In his mind he burst into anger. These Sujans are muttering in the mango orchard alone. She has only one baby rat. He is also playing in the distance. With a few squirrels. They have a good game.

36

On that day, a party meeting was held at Karim's house on Monday. Karim is talking to the leaders. The leaders are again K Karim, Fazlu, Bakul Master Nafiz Doctor and the other two booth participants. And some villagers are sitting. Fazlur's son Sohail is giving coffee to everyone. Nahid is handing out biscuits. Nahid said Dad I will go to town a little now for college trip to get admission in college. There are more friends. Nahid went out to the city to see the college before the result. Will go to Sonarpur. He got on the bus at Thamathampur. He got down at Baharpur and took a bus again to go to Sonarpur. Dad has been lied to. Say college But Nahid has other intentions. What do you mean? He advertised a big jewelery shop in Sonarpur on TV. Cash is said to buy gold. Nahid has been searching the shop for about three hours. But not everyone in the city knows everything. Bella is leaving. Something to eat. Turning around all the time. No food. After going some distance, I found a jewelery shop. He has to eat something before. Entered a large five star hotel. I have never eaten in such a hotel. Thamathampur, Baharpur, Amtala has gone to a better city. I have studied privately but could not eat anything. Where to get it then. Where is the money? All his father's money was spent on his studies. Today he has a lot of money. You just have to redeem the coins. Nahid brought five coins. The waiter came. Gave food. Eat food. It's bad to pay the bill. So many bills. Ten thousand rupees. Where is the money? Grandpa says the hotel owner doesn't have that much money. Take some gold there. The market price which will give something less than that. The owner of the shop i.e. the owner of that jewelery shop is the same. Very happy owner. Oh, you're one. Please point out first. Let's go to the office. The shop owner was shocked to go to the office and show the coins. Is he a big and heavy coin, Mr. I have never seen Cosmin. Said the shop owner. Since when have you been doing this business? Nahd responded cunningly for a couple of years. The owner says that even if you are young, you are a master of these things. What can I tell you then? He measured the coins. About twenty lakhs I can pay. The price of a single coin. Nahid thought in his mind that it might be two or four lakhs. But I don't know the price. Well, there are about one crore, five lakh less days there. If this is the diameter. The shop owner has the same profit and it adds another five lakh rupees. He gave money for cartoons. He wrapped a packet of biscuits in front of Nahid. So that no one may doubt. Nahid then told the shop owner who. Well Kakababu has no house for sale here. Home for sale. I can't say. Well don't do a search. I want to buy a house. Well then do one thing. Call me in two days. I will arrange a house for you. But want a bigger place. All right. Became a good fit with the shop owner. Why not. The deal was to give many more coins. About twenty-five or thirty a month. And why leave such a customer. No matter how much gold is sold or bought in this country, nothing will happen from the government. Gold if lorry lorry You still have a government headache. Your goods are yours. Sure from there. Lots of gold prices here. Why not get less gold here. Then Nahid returned home at night. Leaving money cartoons at home. Mother went to her father's house and told him to give her something to eat. Budd is hungry.

36

Sadeq Matabbar can no longer press Karim. Extremely Sadeq needed two bighas of Karim's land. But now he is gone. New Matabbar. What else can be done to take the land. If uncle wins as a blessing, then he will be defeated. Which must be done before the vote. It cannot be done without the blessings of Nare. She is not alone now. The team is done. Muskil Ray Niyamat. What can be done then uncle. My scar is no longer straight. What will happen to the master's wedding. There is talk of marriage. Will be with Ramadan's daughter. I will come tomorrow with the address from Bilas.

36

In the evening the phone rang on Nahid's mobile. Hello. Who I am a hotel owner from Sonarpur. Oh said. I am waiting for you uncle. Oh so. A house has been found for you. He is asking for about five crore rupees. No problem. You are He will pay the money. I will give you gold. All right. But you have to eat sweets. Of course. Then when are you coming. Not happening tomorrow. Going the next day. Well then. Thanks.

39

The house has been bought. In Sonarpur. Sonarpur is the second capital of this country. Many circles live. The house has been bought. The hotel owner's name was Ali. The man is good. Prudent. Didn't cheat with Nahid. Why would the owner of a lot of money cheat. Hotels, There is jewelry. Owner of crores of rupees. Nahid chose a house. No one is allowed to enter there. Only without parents. Ekchuali is his private room. Of course no one knows that the parents bought the house. With five crore rupees. Nahid came back with everything. About three days later. He spent one night in the new house. What a beauty. Now he owns crores of rupees. Comes home. Bought a car. The market value of the car is around fifty lakh rupees. The people of the village have never seen such an expensive car without a TV screen. A few days ago a car came to the house of Ramzan Matabbar. But not such an expensive car. Everyone is surprised. Nahid is asking many questions. But Nahid said I got in the lottery yesterday. I won the lottery during the examination and brought it from Baharpur today. There is some work to be done again tomorrow. Nahid's parents are very happy. Everyone is happy. Good news before the test results. That's great. Nayana is supposed to win the lottery by phone Says. And offers to grow. Nayana agrees. Within an hour of Sageguje appearing.

Going for a walk in the park. Eating yogurt fluff. Talking. Chatting Just like boyfriend girlfriend. But still the two are friends. Nayana is sitting cross-legged in the park, and Nahid is lying with her head on Nayana's feet. A red rose in Nayana's hand. Picking up thorns one by one. Talking. Well, Nahid, you used to say when I will be in love. So far no boyfriend has come. Hey, come on. Time will tell. You see, we are not lovers, but we are very beautiful. Not so. Hey, there is no benefit in love. There is no such thing as friendship. Of course he is. I haven't found Rina yet. Hey, leave it at that, I don't think about that anymore. I could do it once. Not so. They say rich. And I will not go to the rich. I will get married at the will of my parents. Diameter. Kellafte. What again. I understand. I understand. I realized how easily boys forget girls. Oh so. Rina forgot me. What do I do then. Fingers suck. Need to find out. Hey, where can I find such a big search. And he doesn't look for me. Knows my address. Knows mobile number. Despite that, it has been twenty days since I found anything. He could have given the letter. Didn't do that either. When the girl from the village goes to the city, she becomes madam. And pays attention. Exclude all that. Let's eat something at the restaurant. Let's go I'm hungry too. You still play flute. I play ice cream. I just ate an ice cream. What a mess. What rice again. Hey donkey girl. These are not available in restaurants. Oh, I forgot. Let's go to the hotel. Get up. No. Hold me by the hand and lift me in the style of Promik. Otherwise I will not get up. All right. This is. Diameter. Happy. Really, Nahid, I think you are my friend. What do you think then. Huh ... very close people. True. Wow good. It's been a lot of nonsense, let's go.

Chapter 5

40

Ten days later .....

He went to his house in Sonarpur with all the hidden gold coins. Put some coins in the big cupboard. He dug five sacks of coins on the floor and left them in his room. He did what he had with Terlis again. Parents are very happy to see the building. Dad asked what happened. Nahid said father I will not hide anything from you today. I found five bags of gold coins in one place. And I have done all the work by spending only two hundred from it. Five sacks. That's a lot of things. Dad, today we are rich father. My dream is successful dad. The last day of your troubles, father. Now we all have. I lost my Rina for this money, Dad. Saying this, Dad went out on the street. Strong security at home, Lots of CCTV cameras. The head of state of this Lucia country does not have so many CCTV cameras installed. Nahid is now a big millionaire of the country. But hidden. His only job now is. The company will get approval from the central government. That is why people have been caught. If you have money, everything is available in the palm of your hand. This is what Nahid is seeing now. Nahid has been lacking at home while teaching Nahid all his life. He is not lacking today.

41

The results of the panchayat elections and the higher secondary are also ahead. It is a matter of father and son results. Nahid's parents Nahid all live in the village house. Nahid almost went to town house. Now he has a lot of work to do. Paper ready. There are a lot of problems when it comes to making an industry. There is the matter of rushing. His man said. It will take about twenty days.

42

Rina is sitting on the fourth floor with a girlfriend. The name is Rhea. Very nice to see. There is style. Talk about rubbing salt in my wounds - d'oh! Great body. Chubby. He will raise his hand whenever he sees any boy. Riyao is such a girl. How many have worked with force. Keeps yourself fit. Rina lives in the flat of the pass. That is their flat. Rina's younger grandfather's granddaughter. They are also rich. But the girl is very sweet. She has forced sex with many. Very sexual girl. He did not find a good friend to meet him. The boys in town are just pansy. Nothing can. The work is over after watching the girl all day. But why work. Well, Rina, did you say you love someone? Why. This does not mean that village girls get more. And I don't understand the city. But not real. Yes i know You know I love one too. I don't know what to mean by that. Well, have you ever worked with him? I did. This is how Malta is. Good. How much time has been able to pay. Nothing in your mouth Doesn't stop. Neither you nor I am big. Don't overdo it. You are a high school student. And I'm a high school student. Just a matter of one year. Give me one day. What the heck. Who is your groom Why. Hey, I'm going to visit Dola Bhai. No. Why not. The girl you're looking at. Let me finish. Oh no no. Something will happen. If you hold it a little, it will not run out. Yes. This is why you are so big. I will take a look at this. You know, boys get drunk when they see it. Yes, that's what happens in the city. I will see the time cuts with one of the villagers. Yes, that's what I'm saying. Let the swinging brother go with me. What does that mean? The head has gone bad. Hey sister-in-law, access is not like that. Yes but not at all. Saying this, he started telling stories. If you hold it a little, it will not run out. Yes. This is why you are so big. I will take a look at this. You know, boys get drunk when they see it. Yes, that's what happens in the city. I will see the time cuts with one of the villagers. Yes, that's what I'm saying. Let the swinging brother go with me. What does that mean? The head has gone bad. Hey sister-in-law, access is not like that. Yes but not at all. Saying this, he started telling stories. If you hold it a little, it will not run out. Yes. This is why you are so big. I will take a look at this. You know, boys get drunk when they see it. Yes, that's what happens in the city. I will see the time cuts with one of the villagers. Yes, that's what I'm saying. Let the swinging brother go with me. What does that mean? The head has gone bad. Hey sister-in-law, access is not like that. Yes but not at all. Saying this, he started telling stories.

43

It's been a month since the test. It will still take a long time for the results to come out. It's time for a big holiday. Nahid's father no longer works in farming. People see good and evil. This time many people in the society are raising the tune. After the departure of Ramzan Matabbar, Sadeq is the main Matabbar. This time the gram sabha will be called. Will form a new committee there. Also raised some voices. Sadeq has a bad head. The money of the mosque, the money of Karbala, the money of the society was being eaten. I don't understand that anymore. Where is Sala Karim coming from and sharing everything. I can hear again that he has made his home in the capital. Where did you get so much money from? Still not working. He puts air on his body and walks around.

Sala is killing the road to income from my society in the field. Can't he be removed from the road, uncle? No, it's a blessing. No, we can't do that. Must see another road.

44

The company will be inaugurated in the morning. Work is in full swing. Nahid left in the morning. Multinational Company. Group industry. Not even that can be found here. Big company. Many companies do not order from here. Such a company. Lots of people. There are big company owners and high ranking officers. Nahid or his mother cut the red ribbon in the presence of everyone. Nahid K cut the ribbon and made it sweet. And Nahid fed her parents. The inauguration process of the office lasted till one o'clock in the afternoon.

45

Voting Result Day ....

The results of the Lucia panchayat election today. The whole country has been making noise since morning. What will happen next. The local government has occupied it by force. Because there is a People's Party government in this state. But where the opposition camp is strong, elections have not been held. There are some new faces in the Thamathampur panchayat election. Karim Sheikh, Bakul Master, Nafiz Doctor, Soleiman and Idris. They are supporters of the Socialist Party. On the other hand, Sadeq, Ramzan, Shafiqul and Najib. They are supporters of the People's Party.

Sabir Ali is in booth number one from non-party. The results are being counted. In the panchayat. That's the rule here. In the afternoon. The results have been finalized. The newly elected members became the people.

Booth No. 1, Sabir Ali (Independent Party)

Booth No. 2, Karim Sheikh (Socialist Party)

Booth No. 3, Bakul Master, ("" ")

Booth No. 4, Najib Miah (People's Party)

Idris Ali at Booth No. 5, (Socialist Party)

The fruit announcement is over. The Prime Minister and the President welcomed the newly elected representatives. The people of Thamathampur Panchayat have wiped out the People's Party. Only one member. He was elected from a non-party. The newly elected independent member said he would stay with the Socialist Party. The panchayat will be formed on the next seven days. The newly elected representatives have nominated Bakul Master as the Panchayat President. And Karim Sheikh, the first president of the Socialist Party, will be the co-president. Sabir Ali has been elected from a non-party seat in Ramadan.

46

Ten days after the result of the panchayat election .....

Ten days after the result of the panchayat election, the result of the higher secondary was out. He got Nahid fast bench in the examination. Rina Second Bench. Nahid will study in Sonarpur. Because this time everyone will go there permanently. Will study in the high varsity of the country.

A few hours after the announcement of the results, the phone rang on Nahid's mobile. Recognition number. It is ringing many times. Pretending not to see. Nahid wants to forget Rina. But it is impossible for Nahid to forget that. Still did not receive the phone. Besides, various people of the company are greeting with garlands. Many honors to him. Is he poor now? Time is of the essence.

Rina has been calling all day but there is no response. Today Nahid has a lot of pain in his chest. He also went to the bar and drank wine to forget some sorrow. But where is the more chest pain growing. The pain of love is not to be forgotten. Nahid loves Rina the most in his life. But she doesn't understand why Rina cheated on him. Rina is not such a girl. So did Rina come to town and fall in love with a boy? The risk of sex. It is difficult to say whether or not.

48

A few days later ...

Nahid is walking alone in the park in the afternoon. The environment of the park is very beautiful. Comes to Baharpur occasionally. Because Rina lives here. But Nahid has a hatred for Rina, even though her love for him is hurt. But he loves Rina with all his heart. There is no doubt about it inside the park. Nahid is sitting in the park. Expensive car next door. The price must be around one crore. Smoking. At that time a girl fell while walking in the water of the river in the park. Big river. Deep river. Can't swim. Don't really know. Lots of screaming. But no one is picking him up. Who in the city knows how to swim. Most everyone is scared. Hearing the sound, Nahid went and jumped. Living. The girl is screaming. Very scared. The clothes are wet. Nahid paid three thousand rupees to his driver. To bring a dress. After a while he brought the dress to the girl. The girl went to the caretaker's room in the park and changed. What a shame. This time the girl said. Mr. Come with me. Where in my house. After making many requests, Nahid reached the girl's house. Great house. Big house. The house has two floors. But beautiful. Next to the house is a beautiful four storey house. Old house with many beautiful carvings. Come on. As soon as he went to the bowl, he started shouting. The story has been rumored for a while. It's almost dusk. Let's go to the next house. Come out. Why. Why not. Our home. My grandfather's house. Oh. I don't want to return home late. Why. Stay at our house today. Oh that's good. But you can handle my irritation. What an irritation. Do you have a wife at home? The story continues. Mother called from inside the house. Mommy Mommy. The girl's home nickname is Mommy. But there are good names. Tell mom. You have eaten coffee. Now don't eat rice. Yes, my mother is very hungry. You give us rice, we are coming. All right, Nahid is on the income table. All right, go. He came back to Nahid. Guys, Mr. Let's go. Where. To eat I mean. To eat rice. I don't eat rice now. Oh we eat in the evening. Eat with us today. After much fuss, he agreed to eat. Arabs. So much food aunty. Why Dad didn't like it. No, I don't have the habit of eating so much. I eat less. Well. Dad then do business. Business. My small business. What more can I say. Nahid has heard the name of group industry. Yes, Seto is a big company. That's mine. What said. Your company. Yes, that's right. Wow. So don't give us a tender. Can't get tender. What tender will you take? Mommy's dad knows. We have no business experience. Our company was also doing well. But suddenly the manager flew abroad. Didn't go to law. Went. But to no avail. And he doesn't like our trouble. So I didn't want to involve myself anymore. Take the meat, father. No aunt and no. It is not right to eat so much beef. Mommy, don't get up, Mr. Body Keeps fit. Madam is fit. What's the matter, father? No, I can't eat anymore. Mom said I don't eat either. Let's have a washing machine here. Let's go. Going to the washroom, washing her hands and face, she said, "You know what happens when you eat beef." What happens. Excess leads to sex. Not so. You have great knowledge. Hey girls don't know. Only men know. No, they alone have the right to know. No, it's not. Both of them washed their hands and wiped their faces with towels. But I will not let you return home. Hey, I got into big trouble. Why. No problem. So much for one day. If you were a wife, what would you do? Mom said softly, I used to put it in my breasts. What did you say? No, nothing. I haven't heard. I have heard that you have done a lot. Let's go somewhere again. Let's go. Going to the roof, the two of them are sitting together in a chair, smiling and staring at the sky. Nahid is showing her mother with her fingers on her neck. That's how beautiful the sky is. Where is the cloud going from? Beautiful view. Jonak looks so beautiful all around in the evening. Everything is clear. As if tonight is nine days. At that time the phone came from Nahid's mobile from home. Someone came from the village. Talk on the phone for a few minutes. He puts the phone in his pocket. This mommy let me have work. There is an emergency. All right, go. I will say something like mommy. Said we can't be friends. Why not. We are friends. Then you do it. Yes, of course. Well, you go home and call. And will come tomorrow. Okay, what will happen with Asab tomorrow. There is work. Ok bye Nine days and nights. At that time the phone came from Nahid's mobile from home. Someone came from the village. Talk on the phone for a few minutes. He puts the phone in his pocket. This mommy let me have work. There is an emergency. All right, go. I will say something like mommy. Said we can't be friends. Why not. We are friends. Then you do it. Yes, of course. Well, you go home and call. And will come tomorrow. Okay, what will happen with Asab tomorrow. There is work. Ok bye Nine days and nights. At that time the phone came from Nahid's mobile from home. Someone came from the village. Talk on the phone for a few minutes. He puts the phone in his pocket. This mommy let me have work. There is an emergency. All right, go. I will say something like mommy. Said we can't be friends. Why not. We are friends. Then you do it. Yes, of course. Well, you go home and call. And will come tomorrow. Okay, what will happen with Asab tomorrow. There is work. Ok bye

48

Karim has come to the village. President formed today. Many people in the panchayat. Different opinions are coming again and again. Some people are talking loudly. The panchayat secretary said, "You decide who will be the president." After a lot of pressure, the names of the two were selected. Bakul Master will be the president. Hearing the name of Bakul Master, the party workers caused trouble in the panchayat. Great commotion. In the end, Karim was given the responsibility of president and vice-president. Karim is now the head of the panchayat. Panchayat is the direct development in this country. That is why there is a panchayat office. Here BDO is not prescribed development. The budget is presented in the panchayat. That budget goes to the video. The law that will be passed will run in that area. But except the law of the center and the state. Fun at the party office all day. Eating and drinking in the village. Party Vice President Fazlu says, Today is not the festival of our party, it is the festival of the whole region. Fazlu thanked the people of the area. Parties from the region will also contest the next Senate elections. The rules here are different. Each region has one senator. Happy all day. Returned home at night.

49

Nahid looks back at the house. Hey who are you I don't recognize you. Not you. Yes, I can't recognize it now. You have not become rich. Well, mother, you tell me I can't make fun of him. Well okay don't joke. Saying this, Nahid kissed her gently on the cheek. And put your hand on my neck and say let's go to my room. Why. Hey, who are you here for? No, I came for my aunt. Not so aunty. F f Where. In my room. Mom, you send coffee with Bubai. The two of them walked hand in hand to Nahid's other room. The two went to bed and sat down. Nahid went and made the bed. Now tell me how are you. And tell me how I will be. You are not. There is no Rina. You are both my best friends. Yes. Good news at home. You can do one thing. What work. Admission is not necessary. Yes, Seto is in our college. No, you will be admitted here. Wow, that's good. You don't have money either. I do not have. I am the daughter of the poor, Who knows what will be able to teach in our college. So I can't say. You are not just my friend. You know. We grew up together. I will stay at home. Becoming my friend, I will tell my uncle and aunt. You will not have any problem here. I will do a degree from a big university. The name of the village will be bright. That's what I want. We are poor but have rights to everything. Yeah Al that sounds pretty crap to me, Looks like BT aint for me either. Why. Why don't you do it in high school. Tap water also has to be brought and fed. Oh. But you see, there is no love like ours. Don't tell me. We have so much in common. Okay see you later. The coffee came. Here are some stories of eating coffee. Nahid is sleeping. Nayana said, your sleep pacabhahe you sleep I go to aunt. That's right. And I will not dakis to eat. Why not Khabi. Nayana lived in the village house like her own house and like a daughter. So that's the use here. Everything feels his own. And Nahid's family doesn't care. He loves his daughter even more,

50

Hey, where are you coming from? Yes i am coming It will take a few minutes. Oh, I'm standing in front of the gate. Come on. I'm here, I can see you. Parking there. You know I've been waiting for you for a long time today. That's right. Come on come on. Nahid followed his mother. On the second floor. He sat on the sofa and read a book. The book was sexual. Mom came down after reading the book. Mommy is smiling. After a while he entered the second floor with coffee. Nahid is still reading the book. I think there is a lot of excitement in Nahid's body. Mom left two glasses of coffee and kissed her from behind. Because of Nahid's excitement, He also started kissing hard. And Mommy took Nahid K to bed at one point. Both are very excited. The door was locked when it arrived. The hot coffee is getting cold. There are books lying on the carpet under the sofa. The bed is moving. There is a squeaking sound. The two were then in a state of complete excitement. Nahid is rubbing herself lying on her body like a soft fluffy sponge. Mommy's navel body breasts are getting smaller and getting bigger again. Being the sound of fos fos. Mommy is biting her lip. Mommy is touching her vagina again. Breast abdomen everything is open now. There is nothing left. Butter-like food in front of Nahid now. Just eat it. Nahid ate that Rina and today Mommy. This twice in life. Sex is not something that If there is permission from both parties. Sex is a symbol of absolute love. Nahid is loudly performing a love game. The work of this game lasted for an hour. It's fresh now. He took cold coffee and brought hot. Take this. Hey, you brought coffee again. Hey, if you work hard for so long, eat something. With two boiled eggs. Does anyone eat eggs with coffee? No, but I brought it. No need to eat. Nahid is not ashamed like the village now. It's a kind of resentment to reduce Rina's love. Well, Nahid, tell me where you got so much talent. After eating the egg, he sipped his coffee and said, I never got out. Besides, we are village people. Now I live in the city. Possessing endless money. But then I was ashamed of these sex tex. Didn't have sex. Who did one. True. Maybe that's why I can give more time. Nahid, it is difficult to find a groom or a friend like you. My life has been blessed. You know I can't tell you that I like sex so much. You can use me whenever you want. I will be waiting for your father. Not even the size of your grandfather is huge. The men of the city can't. Weak. Evening while talking. At that time my mother said let's come back from the flat next door. Someone understands either. Yes, it is my little grandfather's house. Oh. Let's go then. Don't say anything. Tell me why. We have a home. You know there's a great stuff in that house. What a figure. Girl's goods or boy's goods. Girl stuff. So don't pay attention. Hey no no what are you saying. Wow what a big house. Such a beautiful house. He entered the house while talking. Entry I had to see the little grandfather, that is, the old man of the house. Hey Riya you. Yes, Grandpa. Who is it Definitely a boy friend. Hey old man, no, you need a boyfriend again. Seto, of course. Take it inside. I will go to my sister's house. Oh. Seeing Didi, you are forgetting me. I go Grandpa. Which. Go brother. As soon as he came to his sister's house, lightning struck Nahid and his mother or rear sister Riner. Here you are. And you. This is our home. There are tears in Rina's eyes. There is electricity between the two. Nahid said to Riya, Riya, get out of here. I don't want to be here for a moment. Why. I don't know why. I don't want to stay, that's why Nahid is coming out. At that moment, Rina said, "Wait." . Why are you leaving to see me? I hate you now. You came to the city and forgot your conscience. You have become stupid. I can't talk to you. And if I had known, I would not have come to this house. Rhea is my friend so I came to visit. Listen to me. It's not my fault. It's all father's fault. Why father's fault. I'm telling you everything.

(Previous story)

Dad came to my house that night, what are you doing mother. I am wondering what else to do, I will call Nahid. I left the village. Who knows what to do. No need to call. I'll give him a surprise. What a surprise dad. I will give him a job after the examination. Will also study with. Then I will take leave with marriage.

Dad promised me so I couldn't communicate. Saying this, he started crying loudly. At that time Rina's mother entered. He was listening to everything from outside the house. Yes, father, there is nothing wrong with him. Depressed all day. I don't eat well. Her father works all day. I don't stay at home. Aunty Assalamu Alaikum. Hi

Dad. Uncle did not understand the meaning of office. Rina's mother tells all the facts. Finally Nahid understands everything. What joy Nahid and Riner. But Riya's mother's heart was completely broken. She got a mind-blowing sex partner. Is the boy handsome? The figure is also beautiful. Fitness body. The two of them wandered around all day. But Nahid never once said he was a millionaire. There are big houses and companies in the capital of the country. He has made progress in such a short time.

51

Nayana was admitted to Sonarpur University with the permission of her parents. Nahid and Nayana have been admitted together. He has also built a house in Baharpur. Five floors. Comes to this house occasionally. Spends the night. Riya was shown this house. The house is located by the river. This house was built to be in a pleasant environment. Rina and Nahid come to visit from time to time but did not show the house. He called today and said the address of the house. Rina came and knocked on the door. There is no one in the house. There are no guards. Shunshan. There are many beautiful works of art from the outside to the inside of the house. Nahid welcomed him and took him inside. In Nahid's room. Nahid came to another room to ask Rina to sit down. The coffee was made in flax. He entered Rina with flax and mug. Nahid said with coffee to Rina, Nao baby. This is for you. Talking while eating coffee. Nahid finished his coffee and sat down on the bed next to Rina. Rina was sitting on the bed with her legs dangling. The sofa was, of course. Rina saw Nahid lying down and said, What matters is why you lie down. Not like that. You tell your story. What can I say again. Nothing to say. How beautiful you really are. Saying this, he started waving his hand. What matters is that you seem excited today. Why not look excited. Maybe. Well, Tina will have the advantage of not showing me the story. Rina has not had sex for a long time. She had her first sex at Nahid's house. Rina lay down on her back. Nahid climbed on Rina's chest while telling the story. It doesn't matter if he does something today. I will not touch. Saying this, he started moving his cheek with a finger. Tickle. Rina keeps laughing. Riner grumbled. Tingling in the legs. Kissing and rubbing, on the navel. Rina burns all over her body. He started rubbing on his chest. It gets hot for both of them. Nahid in the stomach with his hands. Rina's body is puffy. The two of them spent a few hours in bed. In the navel of the throat. Rina burns all over her body. He started rubbing on his chest. It gets hot for both of them. Nahid in the stomach with his hands. Rina's body is puffy. The two of them spent a few hours in bed.

52

The session will continue in the panchayat. The first session of the first panchayat. New members. Everything is new. Newly elected members have appeared in the panchayat. The secretary of the panchayat is the speaker. The rules here are different. Everyone is sitting. Nahid's father Karim is presenting the budget. A few good budgets were presented throughout the day. A law is running. Everyone is giving their opinion one by one. Nahid's father is explaining about the budget. The evening session ended. One week in a row. It is the autonomy of this country.

53

Two years later ......

Today is Nahid's wedding day. Lots of people. Very crowded wedding house. The ceremony is being held in the village. Riner got married to Nahid. Today the two are very happy. Who knows what will happen on the night of the flower arrangement. Maybe something terrible will happen .....

Finished

(Some words)

Dear reader. The book is only the first volume.

Readers are being told the purpose. Maybe the author thinks it's completely rude. But what is happening inside or outside the society at present is only highlighted. There are many such people in our society who are involved in bad deeds. So refrain from these things. That is what is being said at the end.

Thank you